Gwen *and the*
Underwater Sorceress

Gwen *and the* Underwater Sorceress

LISA CARNEHL

Illustrated by Mila Anderson

RESOURCE *Publications* · Eugene, Oregon

GWEN AND THE UNDERWATER SORCERESS

Resource Publications
An Imprint of Wipf and Stock Publishers
199 W. 8th Ave., Suite 3
Eugene, OR 97401

www.wipfandstock.com

PAPERBACK ISBN: 979-8-3852-4632-8
HARDCOVER ISBN: 979-8-3852-4633-5
EBOOK ISBN: 979-8-3852-4634-2

07/14/25

To my beautiful, imaginative, and spunky children.
I love you.

LISA CARNEHL

To my art teacher, Pearl Garcia,
who encouraged me to put myself out there.

MILA ANDERSON

Contents

Acknowledgments

Originally, I wrote this story simply to be a gift to my daughters. My incredibly supportive and loving husband, Adam, read it and encouraged me to submit it for publication. I am thankful for him, his unwavering faith in me, and all the help he gave me along the way.

I would like to thank my family for their support, especially my parents, who were among this book's first readers. I am indebted to my wonderful friends Allie Minami, Laurie Bart, Bethany Bauer, and Parinita Shetty, who read this book with critical eyes and gave me helpful feedback and loving encouragement.

I would also like to thank the inspiring Mila Anderson, who jumped at the opportunity to provide illustrations for my story and brought the underwater city to life.

This book was inspired by my imaginative, beautiful children, especially my eldest daughter, who would give anything to truly be a mermaid.

Earthen, ocean, the two shall be

Rejoined in familial harmony.

Once bonded, the history reversed

Shall finally end the wicked curse.

1

A Voice from the Sea

GWEN LIVED WITH HER parents and her little brother Teddy in a small white and blue house by the ocean. She was tall for a twelve-year-old, with blond curly hair and blue eyes, whose passion was creating art using the natural materials the beach and ocean provided. Her brother Teddy also had blond hair and blue eyes, but he preferred playing in the sand with tanks and army men over doing art projects.

Gwen's parents, Edward and Grace, moved to the quiet house by the ocean two years ago. They used to live in a neighborhood in the suburbs of a large city, where Gwen could visit art museums and attend a big school. While Gwen and Teddy enjoyed much about city life, there was something about their home that made her parents sad, though Gwen didn't know what it was. Her mom, Grace, had only said that she felt drawn to the ocean, and she believed this was where the family was supposed to be.

Whatever the reason behind why they moved, Gwen and Teddy grew to love their secluded home on the sea. In the mornings, they worked on their education with their mom in the little house, but in the afternoons they were free to explore the beach and splash in the waves.

Gwen loved to walk slowly along the shore and look for seashells, fossils, beautiful rocks, feathers, and sea glass. While Teddy played in the sand with shovels and army men, she created fanciful scenes and works of art with all of the treasures she gathered from the ocean.

One sunny summer afternoon, Gwen and Teddy were at the shore as usual. Teddy was digging bunkers for his army men in the sand, and Gwen smiled as she heard him strategizing to himself about where he would set up his line of defense. She breathed in the comforting smell of the salty waves, and decided to look for sea glass for her latest project in the glistening sand where the waves kissed the shore.

Gwen left her brother to his play and carefully made her way down to the water, peering at the ground as she walked. In her head, she could picture the mosaic she planned to create with sea glass and shells of a beautiful mermaid swirling through the ocean. She was smiling to herself, lost in thought, when something glinted at her from the wave that gently rolled over her feet. She blinked and shook her head, not sure if she had imagined it. No, there was definitely something sparkling at her from the sand. Gwen splashed over to the object and leaned her face toward the salty water. Then, she gasped.

"Teddy! Come look at this!" Gwen called out. Teddy looked up.

"What is it?" he shouted back.

Gwen peered closer. "I don't know yet, but it seems to be something amazing!"

Gwen reached her hand into the waves and pulled the object out of the deep sand. She used the ocean water to rinse it off, and then she gasped again.

"Teddy! It's . . . it's beautiful!" Gwen stammered. In her hands she held a shell, but it was unlike any seashell she had ever seen. It was made of delicate gold, and its spiral was encrusted with beautiful pearls. It appeared to have etchings of complex designs on its surface, and despite how ornate it was, it was as light as a feather.

"What is that?" Teddy asked, looking around Gwen's shoulders to get a peek at the shell.

"It's the most beautiful thing I have ever found!" Gwen replied.

"Are you sure you found it in the water? It doesn't look real," Teddy said with disbelief.

"It was right here!" Gwen pointed to the spot where she picked up the beautiful shell. "But you're right, I don't think it was made naturally."

Teddy peered closer at the shell. "Yeah, I think you're right. This must belong to somebody," he agreed. "What are you going to do with it?"

Gwen looked out at the water, and then she looked back down at her shell. "Well," she said slowly, "I don't think I could possibly return it to its owner. I guess I can keep it." She turned the shell over in her fingers with admiration. "It really is beautiful."

As she stood gazing at the shell, her mother's voice rang out from the house. "Dinner time, kids!"

"Okay, Mom!" Teddy called back. He turned to Gwen, who hadn't moved. "Are you coming?" he asked.

Gwen jumped, startled. "What? What did you say?"

"Didn't you hear Mom? It's dinner time," Teddy said, looking at Gwen confusedly.

"Oh, I didn't hear her," Gwen murmured, and squinted her eyes closely at the shell. "Yes, I think I'll take this home with me."

She followed Teddy up the beach, but her eyes stayed on the shell as she walked. It was as though she felt some strange, almost magical connection to the beautiful object, but she couldn't explain what it was or why she felt that way. Despite finding it in the ocean, she knew that it belonged to her.

When she reached the house, Gwen went straight to her room. She opened the door, which was decorated with all of her own original art, and pushed hard to get it open. Dirty clothes, markers, sketch pads, and books filled her floor. As she once told her mother, it was messy to be creative! Her feet forged a path through the clutter until she reached the windowsill, which looked out onto the reflective waves of the ocean. Gwen carefully and delicately set the beautiful shell upon the windowsill.

"That's the right spot for you," she said to the shell.

She paused, and almost expected it to answer her. But, the shell just sat there, glimmering in its golden glory, silent and beautiful.

Gwen stared at it for another moment, and then went to wash up for dinner.

It had been hard for Gwen to concentrate on what her parents were saying and asking during dinner time. Her thoughts kept straying back to the mysterious shell, and she could not understand why she felt so connected to it.

"... and that's why I think I could be in the army when I grow up," Teddy was saying to their dad. "I would know just where to string the barbed wire and set up the machine gun nests!"

Gwen smiled and looked back at her plate as Edward and Teddy talked about "boyly things," a term she and her mother invented when Teddy was just a toddler. She swirled her spoon around, and realized she had barely touched her chicken curry, which is normally one of her favorite dinners.

"Are you alright, Gwen?" Grace asked, looking at Gwen's full plate. "Is something wrong with your food?"

"No, Mom. The curry is delicious," Gwen said, and scooped a big spoonful into her mouth. "I guess I am just distracted by Teddy," she added with her mouth full.

Grace laughed. "That's fine, honey. Just as long as you're okay!"

Gwen smiled at her mom, admiring her curly brown hair and rosy cheeks. She felt blessed to have such a wonderful and understanding mother, and Gwen loved her dearly. Even though Grace had always had a sadness weighing on her, she did everything she could to give Gwen and Teddy a happy and fulfilling life. Gwen wanted to be just like her mom when she grew up.

Gwen shoveled the rest of her dinner into her mouth, chugged her glass of cold milk, and asked to be excused. She kissed her mom on the cheek and went back upstairs to her room.

For what must have been hours, Gwen delicately held the shell and examined it closely. She turned it around and around in her fingers, memorizing every pearl and etching. The biggest mystery to Gwen was that despite finding it in the ocean, she *knew* that the shell was meant to be hers. How that could be, she had no idea.

Finally, she gently placed the shell back onto the windowsill, and propped her head up on her pillow to stare at it. As the sun set outside of her window, she drifted off into a restless sleep, with visions of golden etchings running through her mind.

❖ ❖ ❖

Gwen awakened with a start. She didn't even remember falling asleep, but surely the voice she heard calling to her had just been a dream. Gwen shook her head, trying to wake herself up, and immediately checked the windowsill for the beautiful shell.

It still sat where she had left it, the moonlight glinting off of its golden spiral.

"Gwen! Can you hear me?"

Gwen gasped and grasped her chest. There was the voice again! Was she still asleep? She pinched herself on the arm. "Ow!" she cried. No, she was definitely awake. This wasn't a dream.

"Gwen! Can you hear me, Gwen? Are you there?" The voice was sweet, clearly a girl, but sounded muffled as though it was coming from underwater.

Gwen looked all around her. She was alone in her room. The moon was shining through her window, so it must be nighttime. It was unlikely anyone else in the house was awake.

Who could possibly be calling her? Why did the voice sound so far away?

"Gwen! Please! Answer me!" the voice rang out.

Gwen shook her head in disbelief as she realized the sound was coming from the beautiful shell. How could a voice be coming from it? Was there someone trapped inside? Was it enchanted?

Gwen slowly leaned forward until her face was close enough to see every detail in the shell's etchings. She felt too nervous and excited to say anything.

Once more the voice called to her. *"Gwen! Please, Gwen! Are you there?"*

A cold shiver ran down Gwen's spine, but she knew she couldn't ignore the shell's pleading. Quietly she whispered, "I'm here."

"Oh Gwen! Thank goodness you're there! You can hear me?" the voice called.

"Yes, I am here. I can hear you. But . . . who are you? Are you inside the shell?" Gwen asked.

"No, not inside the shell, but the shell can carry my voice. I'm in the ocean. I have been searching for you! Gwen, please, I need your help! Will you come to the water?" the sweet but muffled voice asked.

"What? The water? You live inside the ocean?" Gwen scratched her head with her hand, half-convinced she was still dreaming. What could this all mean? "I . . . I can't come to the ocean. It's the middle of the night. I have to stay in my room."

"Gwen, this is urgent! If you don't come to help me, all might be lost! Please!"

Gwen didn't know what to do. She instantly felt that she trusted this voice, just as she had immediately known the shell belonged to her. If the voice truly did need her help, hadn't her parents always taught her to help others? But on the other hand, she knew it could be dangerous to go to the ocean at night.

"Gwen! There isn't much time! Please! Will you come to help me?" The voice sounded desperate.

Alright, Gwen decided. *I know what I have to do.*

"I'll help you. What do I do?" Gwen asked.

"Come down to the shore. I will meet you there. Oh Gwen, I knew you would help!"

Gwen quietly slipped out of bed and realized that she was still fully dressed. She grabbed a sweater, slid her feet into a pair of shoes, and went out the door, moving so quickly that she forgot to grab the beautiful shell.

I hope Mom and Dad will understand, Gwen thought as she crept down the stairs. She quietly opened the front door and shivered as the cool night air swept over her face. She took a deep breath, closed the door behind her, and tiptoed to the wide, restless ocean.

2

A Moonlight Surprise

GWEN LOOKED ALL AROUND her as she approached the lapping waves on the shore.

"Hello?" she called out nervously. She didn't see anybody. *Am I crazy?* Gwen wondered. *I am chasing after a mysterious voice from a shell. Maybe this is all still a dream.*

While Gwen was having doubts, a big crashing wave caught her attention. A shape was in the water. It wasn't standing upright like a person, but rather, seemed to be crouched in the water like an animal.

Gwen caught her breath and took a step backward. The moon was behind a cloud, and the shape appeared dark and menacing.

"Gwen?" the sweet voice called out, this time as clear and ringing as a Christmas bell.

"Oh!" Gwen cried out in surprise. The dark shape moved closer to the shore, but she still couldn't tell what it was.

Suddenly the cloud covering the moon moved, and bright light illuminated the shape in the water. Gwen's heart leapt from her chest. The shape . . . was a girl!

"Hello, Gwen!" the girl called out. In the moonlight, Gwen could see that the girl had brilliant blue eyes, a bright smile, and long, tangled blond hair. She seemed to be about Gwen's age, though perhaps slightly younger. She sat in the water, but pushed her body up on her long arms, as though her legs were leaning out to the side. She wore a beautiful purple shirt that was decorated with shells, pearls, and other gleaming sea gems. Gwen instantly felt drawn to this mysterious stranger who appeared to come out of the water. She was not afraid.

"Hello . . . " Gwen said in awe. She took a step closer to the water. "I'm here, but I still don't understand."

The girl pushed herself closer to Gwen. As she did, Gwen gasped and threw her hands up to the sides of her face in shock. When the girl moved herself, Gwen clearly saw in the moonlight that she did not have legs. Instead, the girl had a long, purple, glittering tail!

"You're . . . you're . . . " Gwen stammered, but couldn't bring herself to say the words.

"Yes, Gwen," the girl said, bringing herself even closer. "I am a mermaid."

Gwen shook her head in disbelief. "I . . . I cannot believe it! A mermaid! You're . . . a mermaid! And you're real!"

The mermaid laughed a beautiful laugh that rang across the beach like tinkling bells. "Yes, Gwen. I am a mermaid and I am very real. Just as you are a human girl and you are very real." The mermaid smiled kindly. "My name is Noelle."

"That's . . . a beautiful name," Gwen whispered, still in a state of shock. She slowly lowered her hands from her face and let them dangle numbly at her sides. She had never felt so surprised or confused in her entire life. "I just . . . I don't even know what to say. I never knew mermaids existed."

"Oh, we certainly do exist," the mermaid Noelle said, still smiling sweetly at Gwen. For a moment, the two girls stared at each other, separated only by a few gentle waves. Gwen's mouth hung open, but she couldn't say a word. Finally, Noelle broke the silence and quietly said, "But we might not exist for long, unless you can help us."

Gwen shook herself out of her stupor, and took one small step closer to Noelle. "What do you mean?" she asked.

Noelle's beautiful smile turned down. "Gwen, my kingdom is in terrible danger." Noelle used her arms to push herself closer to the shore and toward Gwen. Gwen also stepped forward so that the water was now lapping at her feet.

"Danger?" Gwen asked, shivering suddenly in the cool night air. "What kind of danger?"

Noelle focused her eyes on Gwen and said, "I live in Sous-Marin, the largest and most beautiful city in the whole merking-dom of Monde Aquatique. It's a wonderful world down there, Gwen," Noelle said sadly, pointing out toward the dark water.

Gwen nodded, but said nothing. Her mind was whirling, but she wanted to listen carefully to everything Noelle had to say.

Noelle continued. "We are peaceful. We protect the creatures of the ocean. We preserve the coral and the reef, and we keep the waters clean. We take care of the elderly merfolk, and we love and tend to the children. We are artists, musicians, and poets. For hun-dreds of years, Monde Aquatique has been a paradise."

Noelle paused and looked with her large eyes at Gwen. "But all of that changed last year."

"What happened?" Gwen asked in astonishment.

"A foul murkiness filled our crystal waters," Noelle said sadly. "Our lovely sea creatures grew sick. The corals began to wither. Nobody knew what had caused the tragedy, and nobody knows how to cure it. I am afraid," Noelle continued, "that our kingdom will perish, as even we merfolk have begun to get sick from the murky waters."

Gwen shuddered, and said, "Oh Noelle, I am so sorry. That sounds terrible. But . . . " she paused, trying to make sense of ev-erything she just heard. "But . . . I don't understand what this has to do with me."

Noelle looked deeply into Gwen's eyes, and said, "I was cho-sen by my people to visit the Oracle of the Grotte Bleue. It was a difficult task, for the blue cave is far from the city of Sous-Marin, and one never knows what the oracle will say. But if it had to be done, and if it could possibly help, I was willing to go on the dan-gerous journey.

"I won't tell you that whole story now," Noelle paused, seeing the look of worry that took over Gwen's face. "But I did make it there safely, and the oracle already seemed to know I was coming!"

"What is the oracle like?" Gwen asked.

Noelle shrugged her delicate shoulders. "I didn't see her very well, as she stayed deep within the shadows of the dark cave, but I could see her flashing red eyes and her flowing white hair. She told me that we were all in grave danger because the Sorceress Mauvais had cursed our waters," Noelle said.

Upon hearing the name Sorceress Mauvais, a cold shiver passed through Gwen's body, though she didn't know why.

Noelle went on. "I didn't believe the oracle at first. I thought Mauvais was make-believe. She was a scary story we were told as children. You know, 'be good or Mauvais just might come take you away during the night.' We didn't think she was real . . . " Noelle drifted off. Her face turned toward the moon, and Gwen could see a pearly tear roll slowly down her face.

Gwen felt her own heart sink as she saw how sad Noelle had become, gazing at the moon, lost in her own thoughts. Gwen waited for a moment, and then gently prompted, "But I guess she *is* real . . . "

Noelle sighed and turned back to Gwen. "Yes, it seems to be true. The Sorceress Mauvais is real, and she has turned her wrath and anger on Monde Aquatique. I don't know why, but her murky curse is slowly killing all life within our peaceful world."

"That's horrible!" Gwen exclaimed, feeling a surge of anger at the thought of a sorceress cursing kind, innocent merfolk. "What are you going to do?"

"That's the same question I asked the oracle. She said I had to find a human girl named Gwen, and she gave me three enchanted objects. One, I believe you already found."

Gwen raised her eyebrows, confused, before she gasped and cried, "The shell! The beautiful golden shell!"

Noelle smiled and nodded. "Yes, the shell was a gift from the oracle. She told me to throw it into the highest wave I could find, and said it would lead me to the human girl. I don't know how it found you," Noelle admitted, smiling. "But that's the oracle's mystery.

"She told me I was to keep the shell's companion," Noelle continued, and held up a smaller golden shell hanging around her neck. "With this, I was able to speak to you from underneath the water, and it somehow steered me toward this very shore."

"Incredible," Gwen exclaimed, shaking her head in disbelief.

"And then she also gave me this," Noelle continued, and held up one of her hands. Gwen could see a shimmering silver ring encircling her pinky, with the same beautiful etchings that adorned the shell still sitting on her bedroom windowsill.

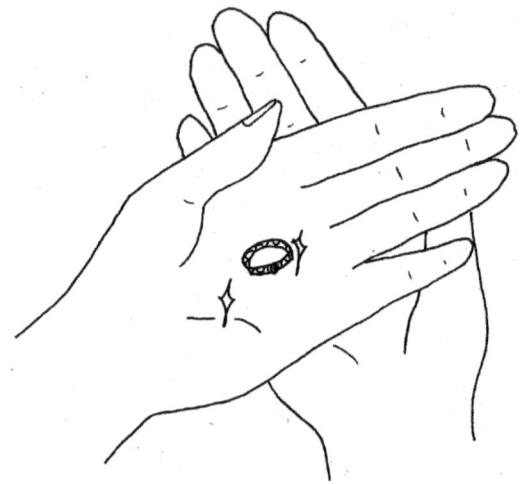

"It's beautiful," Gwen said, looking at the ring.

"Yes," Noelle said. "But it's much more than that. And it's also for you."

Gwen's mouth dropped open. "For me?" She started to reach out to the mermaid, but at the last moment pulled back and threw both hands into the air. "How could the oracle know anything about me? Noelle, I still don't understand!"

Noelle shrugged and gave Gwen a small smile. "To be honest, Gwen, there's a lot I don't understand either. For after the oracle gave me these gifts, the last thing she said was a riddle. She said it was the key to defeating Mauvais and her wicked spell."

"A riddle?" Gwen asked, more puzzled than ever. "What was it?"

Noelle closed her eyes. "I have it memorized, though I still don't understand the meaning. This is what she said:

Earthen, ocean, the two shall be

Rejoined in familial harmony.
Once bonded, the history reversed
Shall finally end the wicked curse."

Noelle shook her head. "And with that, the oracle sent me away from her grotto and told me to call into my shell every night until it could guide me to you."

Gwen stood still. This was all too surreal. A genuine mermaid knelt before her. A sorceress was cursing the seas. An oracle somehow knew who she was, and spoke in mysterious riddles. Gwen was an imaginative girl, but this was more fantastical than she ever could have dreamed possible.

"So now, Gwen," Noelle interrupted Gwen's thoughts, "I am going to ask you to come with me. I don't know how it is that you are to help me rescue my kingdom, but I know we have to try. I can't let my people down."

Gwen looked into Noelle's shining eyes, which were filled with both sadness and hope. Then, she looked back at the dark house behind her shoulders where her parents and brother were peacefully sleeping. "What would my mom and dad say?" she whispered to herself. She struggled with the thought of leaving her family, and abandoning her safe life in her little seaside home.

Gwen stood quietly thinking for a few minutes, then turned back toward the beautiful mermaid. "I want to help you, but I am

15

afraid to leave my family. I love my parents and my brother so much." Gwen chewed on her lip thoughtfully and stared at her toes, covered in the gentle waves of the ocean. "But they always tell me that it's important to help others in need. They want me to do what's right." She looked once more behind her at the peaceful, silent house. "Could doing what's right really be fighting an underwater sorceress?"

Suddenly, a thought struck Gwen, and she quickly looked back at Noelle. "What about your family? Do your parents want you fighting this Mauvais?"

A sad smile played at Noelle's lips. "I have no family; no real family anyway. As a baby, I was discovered floating on a bed of seaweed, and was taken in to be raised by the community of Sous-Marin. I love my people dearly, but I do not have a mother and father that I can remember."

Gwen frowned, and a pit of sadness formed in her stomach. "Oh Noelle, I'm sorry. I shouldn't have asked." She tore her eyes away from Noelle's and looked down at her shoes. She felt more conflicted than ever over the impossible choice she found before her.

Then, she suddenly slapped herself on the forehead. "What am I talking about? I couldn't come with you even if I wanted to!" Gwen pointed at her feet, wet with the ocean's salty water. "I'm a human! I could swim with you a short way, but I could never go down to your kingdom."

Noelle smiled knowingly and leaned in, as the gentle waves lapped over her shining tail. "Have you forgotten about the oracle's final gift?" Noelle held up her finger to show the silver ring, which sparkled mysteriously in the moonlight. "This is not a regular ring. It holds very powerful and secret magic. All you need to do is put it on your own finger and . . . " Noelle gestured to her mermaid tail.

Gwen's jaw dropped again. "You mean . . . " she whispered. "You mean . . . I could become like you? Become a mermaid?"

Noelle nodded and smiled. "For as long as you wear the ring, you can breathe under the water, you can see under the water, and your legs will be transformed into a tail so you can swim through the water."

Noelle took off the ring and held it gently out to Gwen. In the moonlight, it appeared to glow. Gwen looked at it closely. The promise of the adventure of a lifetime was alluring. She was drawn to Noelle and wanted to see her world. But she knew it would be dangerous, and she was afraid.

"Would the change be permanent? Would I have to say good-bye to my family forever?" Gwen asked nervously.

Noelle smiled and shook her head. "No, not permanent. When you take the ring off, you will become a human girl again!" She held the ring closer to Gwen, and her eyes seemed to sparkle with hope. "What do you say?"

3

Going Underwater

GWEN TOOK A DEEP breath, and closed her eyes. She stood quietly for a few minutes, praying for the wisdom to make the right decision and the courage to do what needed to be done. When she finally knew the answer, she lifted her head, looked into the mermaid's shining eyes, and said, "Alright, Noelle. I'll help you." Slowly, she stretched out her hand toward the ring that glowed in Noelle's fingers.

Noelle tipped the ring into Gwen's outstretched hand and said, "Thank you, Gwen. I knew I could count on you! I just knew it!" She smiled confidently. "I believe you will see your home again. Together, we will find a way to stop Mauvais."

Gwen gulped and nodded, hoping she looked braver than she felt. "What do I need to do?"

"Simply slip the ring onto your own finger," Noelle explained, "and the oracle's magic will do the rest." With that, Noelle used her arms to push herself back into the waves until only her head and shoulders were above the water. "Are you ready?" she called out.

Gwen nodded. She stared for another moment at the glowing ring, took a deep breath, and slipped it onto her pinky.

Instantly she felt a little dizzy, and dropped to her hands and knees. She felt an odd sensation in her legs, as though she couldn't help but clasp her knees together. A wave splashed over her face, but she didn't splutter; in fact, it felt refreshing! She opened her eyes and squinted back at her feet. They were gone. In their place was a magnificent tail, with shimmering purple scales and delicate waving fins. Gwen let out a laugh just as another wave splashed up in her face. The water filled her mouth, but she gulped and laughed again. The water felt as natural in her mouth as air!

She heard the ringing laughter of Noelle through the crashing waves. "Come on, Gwen! Come under the water with me!"

Without another look back, Gwen threw her body under the next big wave. The instinct to bounce back to the surface was gone, and instead, Gwen used her powerful tail to propel herself further from the shore. To her great surprise, she could see perfectly under the dark water. The ripples of sand shone brightly, and each sea-shell glinted at her with crisp clarity. She looked ahead of her and saw Noelle clearly, her beautiful blond hair swirling around her smiling face. "I can see you, Noelle!" she cried out, surprised again at how loudly her voice carried.

Noelle laughed her ringing laugh, and gracefully swam right up to the new mermaid. She grabbed Gwen's hand and said laughingly, "Of course you can! You can see, and hear, and breathe just as naturally as if you were on the surface!" Noelle gave Gwen a little tug. "But you'll never truly understand how that tail of yours works until we get into deeper water. Come on!"

Noelle turned her body away from the shore and used her free arm to orient her body downwards. Gwen mimicked her movements, with a sense of excitement filling her all the way to the tip of her waving tail. "Ready?" Noelle asked.

"Ready!" Gwen shouted. Hand in hand, the mermaids swished their mighty and beautiful tails. Gwen felt how powerfully she moved through the water. With each kick, the surface grew faint above them, the sand dropped further below them, and the treasures of the ocean opened up to them. Gwen knew it should be getting darker, but to her mermaid eyes the ocean only grew brighter. She kicked harder and felt how quickly she could move through the ever deepening water. She laughed again and let go of Noelle's hand, reaching out toward a school of glowing butterfly fish. As the fish scattered around her, Gwen swished her body in an underwater somersault. "This is amazing!" she cried, spinning her body two more times.

Noelle laughed and clapped her hands with delight. Gwen spun again, twirling her arms above her head and fanning her tail fins out behind her. A little orange fish passed by her ear, and to her surprise she reached out and caught it in her hand. The fish sat patiently in her fingers. "How did I do that?" Gwen cried out, looking at the fish's bulging eyes.

"The mermaids are friends to the fish!" Noelle laughed, delighted at Gwen's astonishment. "That's a sweet little sea goldie. You can pet him if you like!"

Gwen stroked the glowing fish with her thumb, and it felt as natural as stroking a cat. It might have been her imagination, but the fish even seemed to purr with pleasure. Gwen giggled and opened up her fingers, letting the fish swim away.

As her eyes followed it, she couldn't believe what she could see. The water teemed with fish of all sorts: coralfish, clownfish, bannerfish, herrings, and many others she didn't recognize. She saw seahorses merrily chasing each other through strands of streaming kelp. Her mermaid eyes could even see the plankton floating lazily all about her. How could it be that she never truly appreciated the beauty of the water?

"Oh Gwen! Here are the dolphins!" Noelle's sweet voice rang out, interrupting Gwen's thoughts. Gwen followed Noelle's pointing finger and grinned at the pod of playful dolphins. Their dolphin-laughter filled the water as they bobbed around one another. Noelle swam right to them, grabbing one's dorsal fin and turning with it in a fast corkscrew. The dolphins came up to Gwen, rubbing their snouts along her arms in an invitation to play. Laughing, Gwen swam in circles with the dolphins, bobbing in and out of their formations and latching on to their fins for fast rides.

"I could play with them forever!" Gwen shouted, tickling one dolphin under its smile.

"I know, but they still have to go to the surface, remember? We don't!" Noelle said, and stroked a dolphin along its back. "Time to move on!"

Gwen waved goodbye to the dolphins, who waved their fins back at her and continued their happy play in a different direction.

Still laughing from the exuberance of the dolphins, Gwen exclaimed, "I can't believe it!" She turned another graceful somersault. "I knew the ocean was amazing, but I had no idea it was *this* beautiful!" She spun around to chase after a school of darting fish, enjoying the feeling of being surrounded by hundreds of tiny swishing fins. "What are these called?"

"Those are yellow goatfish," Noelle answered, catching up to her. She stroked one of the fish as it swam past. "They're beautiful, aren't they?"

"Everything is beautiful!" Gwen laughed, and blew at a clownfish going past. A stream of bubbles came out of her mouth, which made her laugh again. "It feels so magical, Noelle!"

"This isn't magic; this is the world God created," Noelle replied, tickling a lined butterfly fish as it went past. "You just didn't have the eyes to see it before!"

"Well, I can see it now! Let's keep going!" Gwen spun again and swam downwards, with Noelle following close behind. The top of a large coral reef peered up at them, the brilliant colors flashing as starfish scuttled over the bumps and knobs. Gwen swam closer, admiring the unique shapes and fluorescent qualities of the corals. She smiled as the fish swam in and out of the secret chambers, and laughed as she watched two shrimp snap their teeny claws at each other. Shadows of a passing bloom of jellyfish danced across her arms, and she drew back as she watched a long eel emerge from one hole and swim into another.

Then, she felt Noelle touch her arm. "I know it's incredible, but we really must keep moving," Noelle said. "It's a long swim to reach Sous-Marin."

Gwen nodded reluctantly, the glow from the corals still illuminating her eyes. She turned and followed Noelle, who swam boldly through the schools of fish. Gwen stroked and tickled the fish as she swam through, smiling at the way the fish were drawn to her fingers. It seemed impossible to imagine that a few minutes before, she had hesitated above the surface, afraid of what might be underneath the dark waves. She had always known about ocean life, but that was different from being a part of the aquatic world. Every fish, every plant, and every animal was stunning. Every color, every glow, and every movement was incredible. The danger of her mission was far from her mind as she reveled in the beauty of the ocean.

The two mermaids swam, with Gwen continuing to laugh with excitement over her new body and the world underwater. She might not have laughed, however, if she had known they were being watched.

Brut and Triste, two of the Sorceress Mauvais's wicked sea serpents, kept their distance from the mermaids. They lurked in shadows and hid behind schools of fish, but they kept Gwen and Noelle in their sight.

"Do you think that's really her?" Brut hissed.

"It seems impossible," Triste hissed back, "but the mermaid has been traveling alone. Who else could that other one possibly be?"

Brut's gleaming green eyes flashed in anger as Gwen's merry laugher filled his ears. "How could this have happened?" he spat. "What are we going to tell Mauvais?"

Triste shook his head and his forked tongue shot in and out of his mouth as he thought. "Well," he hissed, "we could be wrong. After all, it was an earthen girl we were supposed to keep away. Maybe . . . " he trailed off, doubt filling his mind.

Brut darted behind a piece of drifting kelp and turned to look Triste in his eyes. "You don't mean to say we should hide this from her? Do you know what she would do to us if we didn't warn her?"

Triste snapped his jaws and stuck out his tongue again. "You fool! Of course we tell her! I only mean that maybe it's not actually her!" He stuck out his tongue once more and swam quickly away from Brut.

Brut followed, and muttered to himself, "Maybe it's not her . . . " The sea serpents stopped talking, but they didn't stop following the mermaids.

4

Monde Aquatique

"WE ARE NOW WITHIN the realm of the kingdom. Welcome to Monde Aquatique!" Noelle said with a sad smile. The mermaids had been swimming for several hours, and although Gwen still delighted in the incredible sights of the deep water, her excitement had tapered as they closed in on Noelle's kingdom. The glittering sand of the ocean floor was now close enough for them to touch.

As the mermaids swam over a large reef barrier that seemed to stretch on for miles, Noelle paused and explained, "This is the outermost border. I know you've enjoyed seeing the ocean tonight, but I am afraid this is when our mission begins."

Noelle gestured toward the expanse of sea in front of her. Gwen stopped and peered around. So far, the water didn't seem any different. The same kinds of beautiful fish swished around them, and she still tasted the clean saltiness of the water on her tongue. Gwen looked back at Noelle, whose face now wore a worried expression. "What exactly are we supposed to do now, Noelle?" she asked.

Noelle slowly shook her head. "I have done what the oracle asked of me. I found you, and I brought you here. Now, I suppose we have to figure out what the riddle means."

Gwen frowned, her tail swishing slowly as she thought. The words of the riddle floated through her mind. *Once bonded, the history reversed will finally end the wicked curse.* She shook her head and looked again at Noelle, who also appeared to be deep in thought. "How do we reverse history?" Gwen asked. "Isn't that impossible?"

Noelle silently shrugged and began to swim forward again, clearly agitated over the mystifying words given to her by the oracle. She checked to make sure Gwen was following her, and then began to swim a little faster. At last she said in a sad voice, "I don't know. I don't know what we're supposed to do."

Gwen felt the weight of Noelle's sadness, and it hurt her to know her new friend carried the burden of saving her kingdom upon her young shoulders. What chance did a little mermaid like Noelle have against a powerful and wicked sorceress? *At least she's no longer carrying this burden by herself,* Gwen thought, as she watched Noelle swimming in front of her. *I still don't know how I am going to help her kingdom, but I'll do whatever I can to help her.*

After a time of quiet swimming, Gwen finally asked, "Are we going to your city now?"

"Yes," Noelle answered without turning around. "It all seemed to start in Sous-Marin, so I think that's where we should go." She fell silent again and continued leading Gwen over hills of sand and through glittering schools of fish.

Suddenly Gwen gasped. She pointed to their right, where she noticed for the first time what appeared to be an underwater structure. It was a large dome, similar in shape to a seashell, and appeared to be made from hardened sand. It had a small opening at the bottom, and was decorated all over with corals, shells, and even glittering gems. "Noelle, what is that?" Gwen asked, staring at the structure in wonder.

Noelle followed Gwen's gaze and said, "That's just a home! There are lots of merfolk who live outside of the larger cities. Some of them are guardians of our borders, and others are simply farmers and shepherds." Noelle smiled at Gwen's amazement, and continued swimming.

Gwen continued to follow Noelle, but her eyes lingered on the home for a few moments. She thought it was beautiful, so beautiful that it was hard to believe it was a simple home. Her mind flashed back to her own projects still sitting in her room, which used the bits of ocean life that washed up on the shore. She had never known the ocean was hiding such incredibly beautiful art of its own, both natural and merfolk-made. She was curious to meet some other mermaids, but for now she knew it was important to keep going. She turned her attention back to Noelle and the water ahead of her.

After swimming for some time, Gwen started to notice a change in the water. She couldn't see quite as clearly, as though there was a haze surrounding her. The water she breathed in began to leave a bitter taste on her tongue, and there was a faint odor stinging at her nose. She sniffed, and realized it smelled somewhat like rotten eggs. "Noelle, the water is different," Gwen said, cringing at the scent.

Noelle nodded. "Yes, this is the change I told you about. It wasn't always like this." She swished the water in front of her nose as though she was trying to rid herself of the smell. "This is the curse of Mauvais. I'm sorry to say that it's going to get worse as we get closer to my city."

As they continued forward, Gwen suddenly noticed that the fish swimming next to her appeared to be moving slower. She stopped and looked more closely at them. "Noelle, is it my imagination, or are these fish struggling to swim?" she asked.

Noelle brought herself next to Gwen and looked at the fish too. "Yes, Gwen. Our waters used to be crystal clean, but with this murkiness came sickness."

Gwen nodded. "I remember you saying that, but I just didn't expect to see it." She gazed sadly at the beautiful striped fish, who spun in slow, sickly circles in the water. "I want to help them, Noelle."

"So do I, Gwen. So do I," Noelle whispered, and Gwen could see that her eyes were glassy with tears. "For now, we have to keep moving."

Noelle gave Gwen a small tug, and the mermaids continued swimming. Whether it was the murky water or the sadness of seeing the sick fish, Gwen didn't know, but she found herself moving more slowly than she had since gaining her mermaid tail. She forced herself to keep up with Noelle.

Time seemed to be passing slowly, but as they swam Gwen noticed more and more fish moving in the same sickly patterns. The foul smell grew noticeably stronger, and Gwen squinted more frequently to try to see through the hazy water.

"We're getting close now," Noelle finally said. "Soon you'll see the outer walls of Sous-Marin."

Gwen nodded and felt a tinge of nervous excitement in her stomach. She couldn't wait to see the underwater city, but she also felt afraid of facing the danger that awaited her. Would she ever be able to solve the riddle? Would she be able to help Noelle and her people? And, the scariest thought of all, would the mermaids come face to face with the sorceress?

"There it is!" Noelle's voice broke through Gwen's thoughts. She stopped, and looked closely where Noelle was now pointing.

Gwen had to blink several times to be sure of what she was seeing. Rising from the seafloor was a massive wall that appeared to stretch up to the surface. It was beautifully decorated in patterns of glittering gems and shells, though it was clearly made of strong rocks. There were cracks just big enough for fish to swim in and out, but no large creature, and certainly no mermaid, could get past it.

"Wow! It's amazing. But how do we get inside?" Gwen asked, as she swam up to the wall and touched a gorgeous chunk of calcite that glittered at her.

Noelle turned and swam to the left. "There are always guards at different posts of the wall. It is their job to protect the city. They'll let us in. Come on!"

Gwen followed Noelle along the wall, admiring the patterns of stones, minerals, and shells that adorned the massive structure. It reminded her of her own natural art projects, except magnified to an incredible degree. If the wall protecting the city was this beautiful, then she couldn't wait to see the city itself.

They came upon a large round stone in the wall that resembled a door. Looking closely, Gwen realized it had a circular opening in it covered with bars. To her great surprise, a face peered out at them from the other side of the wall.

"Hello!" Noelle called out.

The face broke into a grin, and Gwen could see that it was an older man. He had a bushy black beard with shells woven into it, thick eyebrows, and a crooked nose with a large, jagged scar. Though his face appeared tough, his eyes had a kind quality to them, and he called back, "Is that little Noelle?"

"It's me, Lyle." Noelle swam closer to the window and smiled. "I've returned."

"It's good to see you back safe and sound," Lyle replied, with a genuine smile on his face. "And who have you brought with you?" His eyes turned on Gwen.

"This is Gwen," Noelle said, gesturing for the other mermaid to come closer. "She's here to help us."

"Gee, will you look at that," Lyle exclaimed, looking from one face to the other. "Well, let me get this door open for you." He moved away from the window, and then Gwen watched as the entire round stone swung inward, revealing a large opening that Noelle immediately swam through. Gwen followed, and then turned to look at Lyle.

He was very large, with a massive and powerful blue tail. His chest was covered with armor that had a beautiful spiraling shell engraved on it. His head was covered with long brown hair, tied into thick strands with string. He swung the stone back into place behind her, and she could see how strong and agile he was.

As she stared at the first merman she had ever seen, she noticed that he was staring back at her. "Noelle," he said, "where did you find this Gwen?" He shook his head in amazement. "If I didn't know any better, I would say you could be sisters. Same blond hair, same blue eyes, same purple tail . . . it's uncanny."

Noelle and Gwen looked at each other. Gwen had been so taken aback when she first saw Noelle that she hadn't noticed how similar their features were.

Noelle shook her head, smiled, and said to Lyle, "You wouldn't believe me if I told you how I found Gwen, but she's here to help."

Lyle frowned and pulled nervously on his thick beard. "Well, that's good to hear. Things have gotten worse since you left. Everyone is worried." He lowered his voice and said, "And I have to tell you that we aren't as safe as you think. I've seen them myself."

Noelle's eyes grew wide. "What have you seen, Lyle?"

Lyle hesitated, and then whispered, "Sea serpents. They can get in through the fish passages. The other guards have seen them too. We're trying to keep them out, but they're too sneaky."

Gwen felt herself shudder, and she asked, "What do these sea serpents do?"

Lyle shrugged and pulled on his beard again. "I'm afraid I don't know. We haven't been able to catch one, but we know they're coming in and out. We can't close the passages—there are too many of them. And besides, that would prevent the fish from coming in." He looked around him at the imposing wall. "And that's not all. The sickness has gotten worse too. Noelle, the fish are dying."

Noelle gasped and threw her hands over her eyes. Gwen put an arm around her shoulder to comfort her, though she herself was also shocked to hear this sad news. The pressure to solve the riddle and break the curse pressed down on her.

Lyle looked down at his tail fins. "I'm sorry to have to tell you this, Noelle. And I know you want to get on into the city. But it's not the same city you left. Just be ready."

Noelle looked up at Lyle, whose eyes were filled with worry. "Thank you for letting us in, and I know you're doing all you can to protect us. All the guards are." Despite her tears, she gave him a smile. "It's good to see you again."

Lyle returned the smile. "It's always good to see you, little mermaid. And it's good to meet you, too," he said to Gwen, and gave her a small bow. "Good luck to you."

Gwen nodded and tried to smile, but the sinking feeling in her stomach was growing as she tried to process this new information. Sea serpents? Fish dying? Sickness spreading? What could she possibly do to help?

"Thanks," she said quietly, and the girls sadly waved as they swam away from the wall and toward the city.

5

The Sick City

HAD THE WATER NOT been so murky, she would have seen it immediately, but her vision was blurred by the thick haze. At first, it
seemed as though spindly mountains loomed ahead of her. As they
got closer, however, Gwen could tell that she was actually seeing
dozens of gorgeous towers spiraling from the tops of large ornate
structures.

"This is Sous-Marin," Noelle said quietly. "But its beauty is
being stolen by Mauvais's curse."

Gwen nodded and squinted. Despite the cloudy water, it was
clear that the city was magnificent. The buildings were designed
to resemble seashells, and every tower was beautifully curved and
topped with organic ornamentations. Hundreds of smaller buildings formed a large circle on the ocean floor, while larger and more
embellished structures rose in the middle. The overall shape of the
city reminded Gwen of a wedding cake, as the layers rose to finally
be topped with a rounded building ornately decorated with thou-
sands of sparkling jewels.

"I can tell that it's beautiful, Noelle," Gwen said in awe. She
watched dozens of merfolk swimming in and out of the openings.

"Thank you, Gwen. But there should be fish, and seahorses,
and turtles swimming with the merfolk. Lyle was right. Things
have changed," Noelle remarked with shock in her voice.

Gwen continued to look around her in amazement as she followed Noelle into one of the structures on the lowest level. The
inside was even more beautiful than the outside. The floors were
made of shining marble, and the walls glittered with pearls. Long
benches stretched out invitingly throughout the rooms, covered
with beds of soft moss and seaweed. Wide passageways seemed to
connect the interiors of the buildings, and the merfolk swam freely
in between the rooms.

Suddenly Gwen heard the titter and laughter of dozens of
high-pitched voices. A group of merchildren entered the room and

swam to Noelle, and all of them tried to hug her and talk to her at once. Noelle let out a genuine laugh of pleasure as she hugged them all back.

"We missed you so much!"

"Where did you go?"

"Did you bring us any surprises?" They all called out, their voices mixing in a joyous cacophony.

"I missed you all too," Noelle cried, her eyes soaking up the happy sight of the smiling faces. "And yes, I did bring you a surprise." The merchildren all clapped and giggled. "Look over there!" Noelle pointed to Gwen.

The merchildren all gasped, and their tails fluttered in excitement.

"Who is she?"

"She's beautiful!"

"She looks just like you!" the merchildren cried, and several of them swam to Gwen to hug her too.

Gwen smiled and accepted the hugs. She thought the merchildren were adorable, with their short but glittery tails and their chubby arms and cheeks.

"What's your name?" asked a little girl with starfish in her red waving hair.

"My name is Gwen. What's your name?"

"Coraline," the girl replied with a grin. "Are you Noelle's sister?"

Gwen laughed. "No, but we are good friends. Are you all friends with Noelle too?"

"Oh yes," a boy called out. His stubby blue tail fluttered with joy as he said, "Noelle tells us the best stories and will always play our games with us!" The other merchildren nodded in agreement.

Just then Gwen heard a sharp clap cut through the chittering and fluttering of the children. She turned and saw an older mermaid swimming into the room. This mermaid had a glowing ruby red tail and beautiful black hair, with regal gems woven into her locks.

"Children! There you are! What are you doing in here?" the older mermaid scolded.

"Look, Aunty Delphine! Look!" the little voices cried. The merchildren pointed at Noelle and Gwen.

Delphine gasped. "Noelle! You've returned!" She pulled Noelle into a hug, and then held onto her shoulders to gaze into her eyes. "And you look so weary. Did you find the oracle? What did you learn?"

Noelle shook her head and grasped the hands holding her shoulders. "I did find the oracle, but it's too much to explain now, Delphine. We must gather the council at once and I will tell the whole story."

The older mermaid nodded wisely and said, "I will see to it immediately." She turned to the merchildren and called out, "Children, you must let Noelle rest. Please go back to the round room and attend to your lesson with Madame Florentine."

The merchildren waved to Noelle and Gwen and swam giggling out of the room. The mermaids waved back, smiling. When they finished swimming out of the chamber, Delphine seemed to notice Gwen for the first time. "Who have you brought to our city, Noelle?" she asked.

"This is Gwen. She's come to help us. Delphine, things seem so much worse than when I left," Noelle said, wringing her hands.

"I am afraid that is true," Delphine sighed. "We have lost many fish. Our corals are ill too. And Noelle, our people are also being affected by the murky water." Delphine took a shaky breath and then said, "Odette is sick."

Noelle gasped and cried out, "No!" She buried her face in her hands. "Oh, not Odette!"

Gwen, seeing Noelle's obvious distress, wrapped an arm around her shoulders and held her in a tight hug. She looked with confusion at Delphine.

"Odette is one of our merchildren," Delphine explained. "She is sweet, loving, and kind. She has a natural touch with the fish. Everyone loves her. And this sickness . . . " Delphine paused. "There is no cure. Odette is the first of the merchildren to fall ill, but Noelle, since you left . . . the sickness has already claimed the lives of a dozen merfolk."

Gwen felt Noelle shudder. "Oh Noelle, I am so sorry," she whispered.

Noelle wiped her eyes and looked at Gwen. "We have to stop this, Gwen. We have to."

Gwen squeezed Noelle. "We will. We'll find a way."

Noelle looked back at Delphine. "Gather the council, Delphine. As soon as possible."

Delphine nodded and said, "Come to the High Chamber in two hours time. Everyone will be ready." With that, the mermaid swam quickly out of the room.

Noelle sank onto one of the mossy benches, stretching her long tail out and lowering her chin into her delicate hands. "I just need a moment to rest," she whispered. Gwen perched on the bench beside her and stroked her long hair. They sat for a few minutes in silence.

Finally, Noelle said, "I didn't expect things to be so dire here. Odette sick . . . merfolk perishing . . . the fish dying . . . sea serpents penetrating our city walls . . . And what am I supposed to do?" she cried. "Why didn't the oracle tell me more?"

Gwen shook her head. "It hardly seems fair to you, Noelle. But you have been so brave. You went to the oracle. You did what she said. You found me and led me safely all the way here." Gwen once more looked around the room. "I'm in a real mermaid city.

I never in my wildest dreams thought this would happen." She smiled at Noelle. "And we found each other. I feel as though I have known you my whole life. And I won't let you down."

As Gwen caressed Noelle's hair, she noticed for the first time a mark on Noelle's shoulder. It was small, hardly the size of a nickel, but had the distinct shape of a small fish.

"Noelle, what is this?" Gwen asked, lightly touching the mark.

Noelle sniffled and said, "I don't know. It's always been there. I think it was a birthmark. My own little fish." Noelle sighed deeply. "It doesn't matter. I only wish I knew what to do . . . "

The girls rested in silence for a few minutes. Gwen continued stroking Noelle's hair as she listened to the little mermaid quietly cry. She was determined to help, and hated seeing Noelle's distress, but she still couldn't make sense of the oracle's riddle. On the other hand, would the oracle have gone through the trouble of bringing her here if there was truly nothing she could do?

Feeling a renewed sense of optimism, Gwen suddenly leapt from her seat. Noelle, surprised, sat up. Gwen grabbed her hands and pulled her up from the bench. "Noelle," Gwen said, "we are going to figure this out together. We won't let anything happen to Odette or anyone else in your city!"

Noelle smiled at Gwen. "Well, you are certainly one of the bravest souls I've ever met."

Gwen smiled back at her. "I could say the same thing about you. Now, this council. What do we need to do?"

Noelle rubbed her eyes with her hands, shook her tail, and said, "I'll tell you while we travel. Come on." She turned and swam toward one of the tunnels. Gwen followed her.

As they swam through the city, Gwen tried to concentrate on what Noelle had to say, but the beauty of the city was distracting. Despite the haze in the water, it was clear that the city was a gorgeous maze of passages and channels connecting countless large chambers. Every room and tunnel had been decorated with care. The city seemed to Gwen to be one giant love song to the ocean it was built in.

"The council is the group of the oldest and wisest merfolk in our city," Noelle was explaining as Gwen followed her through the twisting tunnels. "They uphold our city's laws. They are fair and just. They love our people and offer guidance to us. It was the council who sent me to the oracle." Noelle turned into a large round chamber with blue mosaic patterns on the floor and ceiling.

"So you are meeting with them to see what they think about the oracle bringing me to you?" Gwen asked as they swam upward to a large hole in the top of the chamber.

"Yes," Noelle answered, swimming through the hole and entering into a long passageway covered with pearls. "If anyone can help uncover the meaning of the oracle's riddle, it will be them. But I fear telling them about Mauvais. I hope they believe me."

At the mention of Mauvais, Gwen shuddered. "They'll believe you. Of course they will." Then she said quietly to herself, "But I only hope they can help . . . "

The two mermaids continued swimming upwards through the city until they reached the very top: the High Chamber.

Brut and Triste darted past one of the mermen guards and dashed out of a crack in the wall, back into the open ocean.

"Mauvais will not be pleased," Brut hissed. "Not pleased at all."

Triste snapped his jaws. "The mermaids are one step ahead of us. But they will never succeed. Not once Mauvais comes."

"Yes," Brut snickered. "Yes, she'll come. Oh yes, she'll come."

The wicked sea serpents sped through the murky water toward the darkest, deepest cave on the ocean floor.

6

The High Chamber

As Gwen and Noelle waited in the outer chamber for the council to finish gathering, a kind young mermaid with soft brown eyes and a pink tail offered them a tray of food. "Surely you must be hungry," the girl said, giving them a gentle smile.

Noelle smiled and replied, "Thank you, Simone. Peace to you." She bowed her head to Simone and touched her fingers to her lips.

Simone set the tray on a marble table and returned the gesture to Noelle. "And to you," she said, and swam from the room.

Noelle turned to Gwen. "I bet you're starving! And you have yet to taste mermaid food!" She gestured to the tray.

Gwen swam closer and suddenly noticed the growling in her tummy. Her eyes tried to take in the feast that was set before them. Beautiful rolls of rich green seaweed contained bright orbs of sea fruit. Delicate white strands of carrageen moss ornamented the tray, encircling piles of sea beans and deep red dulse. Gwen felt her mouth water as she breathed in the fresh smell of the mermaid food, which managed to cut through the murkiness of the water.

Noelle couldn't help but laugh as she watched Gwen's eyes grow wide. "It's not just for looks. Go ahead! You need your strength."

Gwen said a prayer of thanksgiving for the meal and began trying one of everything. The sea beans had a wonderful crisp snap, and the dulse had a deep savory flavor. The carrageen moss tasted deliciously salty, and the sea fruits were sweet and refreshing. As Gwen ate, she felt her mind growing clearer and strength returning to her mermaid tail.

Noelle also seemed to regain the color in her cheeks as she ate. "Mmm," she murmured. "I haven't had food prepared in Sous-Marin in many weeks. You won't find finer chefs anywhere under the sea!" She licked her lips and then patted her stomach. "Even with this foul stench in the waters, I feel much better."

"Me too," Gwen agreed, finishing her last piece of seaweed. "That was definitely what we needed."

At that moment the giant door leading into the High Chamber swung open. A regal merman appeared in the entrance and said, "The council will see you now."

Noelle took a deep breath and nodded. "I'm ready," she said to Gwen, and swam boldly through the door. Gwen followed, though she swam much more timidly than Noelle. She prayed that the council would have the answers the two girls so desperately needed.

Gwen nearly gasped as she passed through the door. The High Chamber was breathtakingly beautiful. The floor was decorated with multicolored gems arranged in a perfect spiral, and the walls were covered in mosaics of ocean life: whales, fish, seahorses, lobsters, and every other conceivable animal. The round ceiling was encrusted with the image of a magnificent seashell matching that which Gwen had seen on Lyle's breastplate, but made from delicate pearls. Arranged in a semicircle in the front of the round room were seven benches covered with lush moss, and on each bench rested a merman or mermaid.

Gwen noticed that these merfolk were older. Their faces were wizened with wrinkles, and beautiful gray hair cascaded down their shoulders. They were dressed in simple purple robes, and though they commanded respect, their eyes were kind.

Noelle swam into the center of the room and bowed to the row of council members. Gwen did the same. When she straightened up and looked at the council, she noticed warm smiles on their faces.

The merman seated in the middle bench spoke first. "Noelle," he said, "we are eternally thankful to see you safely here before us. We knew the task we set out for you was challenging, but you have proven that our judgment was correct." He smiled kindly at her, then nodded deeply to Gwen. "And we welcome you, Gwen, as an honored guest in our city."

"Thank you, Auguste. It was hard, but I found the oracle, and I did what she asked of me," Noelle replied. She paused, looked at Gwen, and then turned her eyes down at the floor. Hesitatingly, she said, "I am afraid the news I bring is bad. I hardly even feel I can bring myself to tell you."

Gwen saw the council mermaid seated in the fourth bench gently shake her head as she said, "This is a place of light and truth, Noelle. You need not fear."

Another council merman added, "Indeed, Noelle, it is hardly possible to surprise us. Summon your courage, and speak freely to us." He smiled.

Gwen was surprised at how comfortable the council made her feel. She had expected to see stiffly regal and unapproachable merfolk, but instead found them all to be kind and compassionate. They knew the danger their city was in, and yet they took the time to comfort Noelle. Gwen instinctively felt she could trust them.

Gwen nudged Noelle with her arm. "It's okay, Noelle," she whispered. "You can tell them everything."

Noelle swallowed past the hard lump in her throat and said in a quiet voice, "The oracle told me . . . that the Sorceress Mauvais has put a curse on our city." She looked up to see the reaction on the council's faces.

To her surprise, she saw understanding nods and sympathetic looks. "Did . . . did you already know?" Noelle stammered.

The mermaid sitting to the left of Auguste spoke. "Though we did not know for certain, we all suspected that Mauvais alone would have both the power and the malice to put such a foul curse upon our waters." Her emerald eyes looked kindly down at Noelle, who gaped back. "Your bravery in visiting the oracle has confirmed our suspicions. We are thankful you took on this necessary task."

Noelle shook her head in disbelief. "How could you have known? I didn't even think Mauvais was real! None of us did!"

Another council merman lifted his hand up to quiet Noelle, with his palm facing the bewildered little mermaid. "Yes, Mauvais is real. She doesn't often show herself, but she's nearly as old as the ocean itself."

"She is?" Noelle gasped. She looked at Gwen, who was just as taken aback as she was. Gwen saw both confusion and fear in Noelle's eyes.

The same merman nodded. "Yes, Noelle. She was one of the first mermaids who swam the beautiful crystal waters of this kingdom, when all of the sea life was new and the ocean was teeming with treasures to explore."

Another council member, a mermaid with deep brown eyes, continued the story. "It was a wonderful time, the beginning of all things," she said. "The merpeople were created as guardians and caretakers of the water. They were meant to live in harmony with the fish, the coral, and plants. And as you know, Noelle, that is still our way. We love our creator, we love each other, and we love our ocean."

Noelle and Gwen both nodded, trying hard to process the new information they were being given.

"There were years of peace and wonderment as those first mermen and mermaids explored and cared for the underwater world they had been given," the council mermaid continued. Then her face fell. "But there was one mermaid who was not content to be a caretaker of the fish. She wanted to rule over the fish, and for that matter, the other merfolk."

Noelle's mouth dropped open. "She wanted to rule? What would make her think she could do that?"

"Pride, of course," answered Auguste's deep voice. "Pride is always at the root of such things."

"Indeed," continued the mermaid with the emerald eyes, "she thought she could do everything that our creator could. And so she sought to become the queen of the sea, and demanded that the other merfolk worship her as such. But she used cruelty, not love, to establish her reign."

"Did it work?" Gwen asked, horrified.

The council mermaid shook her head. "No, Gwen. It could never have worked. After a time of darkness and chaos, Mauvais was cast out of the Monde Aquatique. She was punished for her pride, and was banished to the dark depths of the ocean."

"Did she ever come back out?" Noelle asked in a trembling voice.

Another council merman nodded gravely. "Mauvais has never been completely silent. For a time, she ventured from the depths, trying to tempt merfolk into her service with false promises of power and wealth. But only the sea serpents gave in to her temptations, and have been in her service for centuries."

The brown-eyed mermaid gestured around the beautiful High Chamber. "But this city, Noelle," she said, "this city is the heart of Monde Aquatique. It has always been protected from Mauvais's wickedness. And I don't mean simply our outer wall. I mean that the love of truth and the light of goodness have held her darkness at bay. As long as Sous-Marin stands, Mauvais has no control over Monde Aquatique."

Auguste nodded again. "Yes, Mauvais has been quiet for many years—so many years that you thought she was a myth. But she has not been idle." He frowned. "She has been practicing her dark magic, and now she has found a way to permeate our barriers. Something happened, something changed, to allow her to curse our waters. But we do not know what."

"And it's getting worse," the emerald mermaid interjected. "For as her curse holds, fear and doubt fill the minds of merfolk who once knew only joy and hope. And as fear grows, Mauvais's influence and power grows. It will be only a matter of time until she can freely enter into our city and fulfill her dark plans."

A silence filled the chamber as this somber realization settled over Gwen and Noelle. Gwen was horrified by the thought that she herself had brought fear and doubt with her into this city. What if by coming here she actually helped Mauvais, instead of helping Noelle and her people? Though she tried to fight it, she felt her fear tugging at her heart.

"And so, Noelle," Auguste's voice broke the silence, "we needed to know the truth. And we didn't choose you at random to visit the oracle. Your name was spoken to us in dreams. Somehow, you are connected to Mauvais and her curse."

"Me?" Noelle asked, shocked. "I couldn't possibly have anything to do with it!" Her cheeks flushed bright red. "I would never follow Mauvais. I love this city and our people!"

Gwen saw the sympathy in Auguste's eyes, and patted Noelle's arm. "They aren't accusing you of anything, Noelle. They of course know you didn't do anything. That's not what they mean."

Auguste nodded. "Gwen speaks the truth, Noelle. We don't understand the connection, but we know it exists. Now, continue with your story. What else did the oracle tell you?"

Noelle was flustered, but recounted to the council the oracle's instructions to find the human girl named Gwen. She repeated the mysterious riddle, and she told the story of using the enchanted shells to beckon Gwen to the ocean and the ring to transform her into a mermaid.

When she finished her story, the council sat quietly, but all of them looked back and forth at the two beautiful blond mermaids before them, their eyes shining.

Finally Auguste spoke in his deep, commanding voice. "The riddle is the key to the curse, you say." He smiled thoughtfully as he repeated the oracle's words to himself. "*Earthen, ocean, the two shall be rejoined in familial harmony. Once bonded, the history reversed shall finally end the wicked curse.*" His eyes twinkled.

"Yes, that's what she said," Noelle nodded, confused by the look of hope in Auguste's eyes. "But I haven't a clue what it means. I think . . . "

But Noelle did not have a chance to finish her thought, for at that moment the door to the chamber burst open and the guard rushed inside, panting. "The wall!" he cried. "The wall has been breached! We are under attack!"

7

The Serpents Strike

GWEN AND NOELLE SHRIEKED and threw their arms around one another. The members of the council all leapt from their benches and began giving instructions to the guards, who filled the room.

"Secure all of the children in the inner safe-chamber," Auguste's booming voice called out. "All mothers, teachers, and nurses are to go with them and care for them. Charlotte and Christine, see that it's done." Two of the council mermaids nodded and hastily swam from the room with one of the guards.

Auguste turned to another council merman. "Pierre, go take command of the guardians. Wherever the wall has been penetrated is the most vulnerable, and we must secure the city at that point."

Pierre nodded and left the chamber with two of the guards.

"Henri and Ferdinand, sound the alarm and gather our forces," Auguste then said to the other two mermen. "Take whatever is needed from the armory and distribute our men throughout the outermost structures. Go." The two council mermen nodded and also swam hastily from the High Chamber with the remaining guards.

The final council mermaid, with the emerald eyes, then spoke to the two trembling mermaids huddled on the chamber's floor. "And you two, you need to get to a safe place. Mauvais, if it is she, must not find you."

Auguste nodded. "Constance is right. Go now, and join the others in the safe-chamber."

Constance helped the girls to rise from the floor, squeezing their hands comfortingly. "And remember, the power to break the curse is within you. You must solve the riddle."

Noelle couldn't speak, but gave a shaky nod.

"Do you know the way, Noelle?" Auguste asked.

"Yes," Noelle answered in a whisper. "Yes, I know the way."

Constance pushed them toward the chamber's door. "Then go, with all haste. And whatever you do, do not let Gwen out of your sight." Constance kissed Noelle's cheek, gave a final nod of encouragement, and then turned back to Auguste. As the girls swam out of the High Chamber, they heard the sound of the two remaining council members speaking in hushed tones.

Noelle gripped Gwen's hand tightly as they swam back through the outer chamber and into the passageways of the city. "We have to move quickly to make it to the safe-chamber before the doors are secured," she said shakily.

Gwen swished her tail with all her might, squinting to see clearly through the murky water. For a few minutes, the girls swam without speaking, holding tightly to one another and darting through the hazy passageways. Occasionally a group of mermen would swim past them, holding spears and shields and wearing grim looks on their faces. Gwen knew they were heading to the outside of the city to face whatever dangers awaited them.

As the mermaids swam through a pearl-encrusted passage, Gwen suddenly heard the distinct sound of a child crying. "Wait!" she shouted, and tugged on Noelle's hand. They stopped swimming, and Noelle looked at Gwen with confusion. Then, she heard the cry again. "That's a child crying, Noelle!" Gwen said.

Noelle nodded, and swiveled her head around as she tried to figure out where it was coming from. Another piercing cry rang out from behind them. "That way!" Noelle turned around and swam back in the direction from which they had come. She opened a small door in the passageway and burst into the room, with Gwen following close behind.

Gwen gasped. A screaming merchild crouched in the corner of the room, her arms held above her head to fend off the vicious sea serpent that swam menacingly around her.

"Leave her alone!" Gwen immediately cried. The sea serpent's body whipped around in the murky water, and its glinting eyes looked upon the two blond mermaids in the doorway. Its mouth turned up in a wicked smile, and without saying a word it darted past them and sped down the passage.

Noelle clutched her chest as the serpent swam past her, and then rushed to the merchild. Her chubby cheeks were splotchy from crying, and she had several deep scratches on her arms from the sea serpent's teeth. Noelle caressed the merchild's face and said, "Shh, shh, it's okay now. The serpent is gone."

As Noelle comforted the merchild, Gwen heard a faint moaning. She looked all around her before she realized it was coming from behind the door. She quickly swam to the entry and pulled the door slightly back. Lying on the floor was an older mermaid, who had the same glossy auburn hair as the merchild. Gwen figured it must be the child's mother, who had clearly been knocked unconscious by the swinging door when the serpent first burst into the room.

Gwen knelt down and gently touched the mermaid's head. Her eyes fluttered, and then opened, and she moaned again. "Rosalee . . . Rosalee . . . " she whispered.

Gwen caught the mermaid's grasping hand and said, "Rosalee is here. She's safe."

The mermaid coughed and tried to sit up.

"Whoa, take it slow," Gwen said, and helped the mermaid into a sitting position.

"Rosalee?" the mermaid called out as she leaned on Gwen's arm.

The merchild cried, "Mama!" She pulled away from Noelle's embrace and swam across the room to where her mother sat on the floor. "Mama, oh mama!"

Tears swelled in the mermaid's eyes as she pulled her daughter into her arms. "Rosalee, thank God you're okay. Oh, thank you, God!" she cried as she buried her face in Rosalee's hair.

"She's alright, but she did get some cuts from the serpent," Noelle said, kneeling down beside them. "They must be bound, but first we have to get to the safe-chamber. I don't know how long it will stay open."

The mermaid nodded, still clutching her merchild to her chest. "Yes, we must go. I heard the alarm and we were preparing to leave when the door flew open and knocked me down. It . . . it was a serpent?"

Gwen nodded gravely and said, "Yes, and there are surely more of them. We *have* to go. Do you think you can swim?"

The mermaid pushed herself up, still grasping her daughter. "Yes, we can move. We must."

Noelle grabbed the mermaid's free arm and helped her the rest of the way up from the floor. Rosalee whimpered, but clung to her mother. Her little tail fluttered as they carefully swam around the door and out into the passageway. The water was thick with haze, but the girls didn't see any movement.

"I think it's clear. Let's go," Noelle said, and led the group through the tunnel. Gwen swam behind the others, making sure Rosalee stayed firmly in her mother's arms.

They turned a sharp right and continued into a passageway streaked with opals. At the end, Noelle led them into a large open chamber filled with high shelves of scrolls and rows of smooth benches. Gwen assumed it must be a library or record room of some kind. They hurriedly swam through the aisles, heading for the door at the end of the room.

They were nearly to it when a hissing laugh sounded behind them. Gwen looked back over her shoulder to see a den of serpents glide into the room. "Noelle!" she shrieked.

Noelle looked back and gasped.

Rosalee's mother let out a moan of anguish, and clutched her child tighter. "What do they want with us?" she cried.

Noelle shook her head. "I don't think it's you. It's us." Her eyes widened with fear as she saw the serpents closing in on them.

Gwen shoved the mother and cried, "You go on! You must get Rosalee to the safe-chamber. We'll distract the snakes!"

"Yes," Noelle agreed. "Do you know the way?"

The mother nodded, and said, "Thank you, girls. Thank you for saving my daughter." She bowed to the mermaids and then swam as quickly as she could out of the room and to the right.

"Come on!" Noelle grabbed Gwen's hand and pulled them out of the room, turning to the left.

"We'll never outswim them. We have to find a place to hide!" Gwen panted, kicking her tail with all her strength in an effort to keep up with Noelle.

Noelle gulped and glanced behind them. The serpents had yet to enter the passageway. She looked all around and saw a small open hole in the ceiling up ahead of them. "Up here!" she said, and pulled Gwen into the small opening. The girls found themselves in a small room, which was piled with crates, old rugs, and broken benches.

"Quick, we have to cover the hole!" Noelle whispered, and glanced around. She swam to a pile of thick rugs woven out of deep blue sea grasses. She grabbed one side, and Gwen came to grab the other. The mermaids hauled the rugs over the hole, sealing them inside.

Their hearts pounded in their chests and they clasped hands as they tried to listen through the rugs, praying that their hiding place had not been spotted by the serpents.

Gwen looked at Noelle with wide eyes as she heard the distinct sound of hissing below them. She silently squeezed Noelle's hand, and Noelle squeezed back.

"I know they came this way," a wicked voice below them hissed.

"They can't have gotten far," another voice snapped. "Check all of the rooms as we go."

The mermaids trembled as they heard the sounds of doors in the passageway opening and closing and serpents hissing in disappointment.

"Fools! How could they have escaped from us?" spat a particularly nasty voice. "She'll have our tongues if they got away."

Suddenly, both Gwen and Noelle felt a cold chill pass over their bodies. They shivered, and their trembling increased. A fear neither of them had ever known crept into their hearts, and they clung to each other desperately.

"Yes, she will," they heard a voice say. It was a voice unlike any they had ever heard. It was deep, and yet at the same time shrill and piercing. With those three words, Gwen felt her heart stop, and a panic rose from the pit of her stomach.

Noelle said nothing, but her lips formed the shape of a silent word: *Mauvais.*

8

The Underwater Sorceress

Gwen trembled as she realized that Noelle must be right. Directly underneath them, separated only by a small pile of rugs, was the wicked sorceress herself. There was no other explanation for the fear and panic that she felt upon hearing the voice.

The mermaids clutched each other, too frightened to move, and unable to think.

"We know they came this way, my lady," one of the serpent voices hissed. "We were so close. We almost had them!"

"Almost is not acceptable," the voice of Mauvais again cut through the rugs and filled the mermaids' ears. "You don't realize what is at stake here."

"S-s-s-s-sorry, my lady," a different serpent stammered. "We'll find them."

"You slimy little fools!" Mauvais shrieked, and Gwen heard a thumping sound. "Unacceptable! I will find them myself!"

With those words, Gwen felt panicked. She glanced around the room. It was clearly an old storage room, but there had to be another door. The crates and benches were too large to have come through the hole in the floor. Fighting her crippling panic, she mouthed to Noelle, *We have to get out of here.*

Noelle's eyes were wide with terror as she heard the further sounds of bangs and thumps and exclamations from Mauvais in the passageway below them. But she managed a small nod, and also began to look around the room. The cursed waters made it difficult to see, and there was junk piled high throughout the entire chamber. But as Noelle looked carefully, she noticed a crack in the wall that could potentially be the hinge of a door. She tugged on Gwen's hand and motioned to the wall.

Gwen gulped. She had trusted Noelle until this point, and knew she would trust her to the end. Though her entire body felt paralyzed with fear, she fought through her terror to push herself up. The girls slowly and silently glided through the cramped room, being careful not to bump into anything, and made their way to the wall.

Gwen bit her lip in frustration. It was definitely a door, but it was blocked by a large stack of crates. The girls paused, straining their ears. They didn't hear anything coming from below, but they were also much further away from the hole in the floor. They knew they had to try.

They made eye contact and nodded. Carefully, each mermaid took hold of one side of the first crate. "One, two, three," Noelle whispered, and they lifted the crate. It was heavy, but the girls could manage to lift it and set it on the floor away from the door. A faint smile of relief played at Noelle's lips as they went back for the second crate. They moved it in the same way, and then moved another one. There were now only two more between them and the door.

As they gripped the next crate, they suddenly paused as they heard the rustling of the rugs on the floor. "What's up here?" a serpent voice hissed.

Gwen and Noelle looked at each other, seeing the fear each felt mirrored in the other's eyes. They hastily pulled up the crate, but in their panic they dropped it with bang.

"My lady! There's something up here!" the serpent hissed, and the rugs covering the hole began to move.

"Quickly, the last crate!" Gwen whispered, and the girls grabbed the corners of the final box and shoved it aside. Noelle gripped the round, pearly handle of the door and yanked.

"Faster, you fools!" Mauvais's voice cried out just as the mermaids slipped from the room and slammed the door shut behind them.

They found themselves in another passageway, and Noelle squinted through the murk as she tried to find her bearings. "I . . . I don't know where we are, Gwen. I'm so scared," she whispered, shaking.

Gwen grabbed her hand. "Then we just have to move! We can't stay here!" Gwen pulled hard on Noelle, who seemed frozen in fear and confusion.

"How . . . how could she have gotten into the city?" Noelle murmured as she allowed Gwen to lead her down the passageway. "Why is she doing this to us?"

"I don't know, Noelle, but we *have* to swim! Come on!" Gwen kicked her tail and looked back over her shoulder. She knew that Mauvais and her serpents couldn't be far behind.

The mermaids held hands and darted down the twisting passageway. They cut through a coral chamber and into another tunnel that wound upwards.

Noelle shook her head. "I don't think this is the way to the safe-chamber. These are private quarters," she said. She stopped swimming.

Gwen looked around in panic. "Noelle, we can't stop. We have to keep going, or she'll find us." But Noelle couldn't move. Her fear had completely overwhelmed her. From behind them, they heard the cruel sound of a woman's laughter. Gwen again felt the cold shivers pass through her body that could only mean Mauvais was near. She quickly looked around, realizing they were in a corridor filled with doors.

"Noelle, *move!*" Gwen cried, and yanked her toward the closest door. They shoved it open and slammed it behind them, leaning their backs against it. Gwen looked around, and saw that they were in a bedroom. There was a four-poster bed draped in a delicate seaweed canopy and a beautiful dresser carved out of driftwood, with large pearls for knobs. Gwen pointed at it. "We need to move that in front of the door."

She pulled Noelle again, and swam to the dresser. With her first shove, the dresser didn't budge. "Help me, Noelle!" Gwen cried. Noelle seemed to shake herself awake, and put her shoulder against the dresser. "One, two, three, push!" Gwen grunted and kicked her tail with all her might. With adrenaline pumping through their veins, together, the mermaids somehow pushed the heavy dresser until it rested in front of the door.

They slumped to the floor, panting from the effort. Noelle looked at Gwen, her face filled with sorrow. "I'm sorry, Gwen," she whispered.

"For what? This isn't your fault," Gwen said, seeing the look of pain on Noelle's face.

"Yes, it is," Noelle moaned, tears welling in her bright blue eyes. "I should never have brought you here. The oracle must have been wrong. There's nothing two little girls like us can do to fight a sorceress like Mauvais. There was nothing we could do except run and hide from her." Noelle stared helplessly at the floor.

Gwen put her arm around Noelle's shoulders. "I'm not sorry you brought me here," she said gently. She felt tears stinging her eyes, and gave Noelle a squeeze. "I know we're in trouble right now, but I also wouldn't trade this for anything. I'm so thankful you found me, Noelle. I feel . . . I feel as though I've been searching for you my whole life."

Noelle leaned her head against Gwen's and heaved a shaky sigh. "I know what you mean," she whispered. "But that's why I wish you weren't here. I wish you weren't in danger."

The mermaids held each other and cried, each sensing that there was nothing more they could do to stop the sorceress and her wicked sea serpents. Gwen felt completely helpless, and her heart broke knowing she could not save Noelle and her beautiful city.

As she sat with her back against the dresser, crying with fear and grief, Gwen felt the cold shivers begin again, the sign that Mauvais was near. However, at that moment, she also thought she heard a faint voice calling out.

"*Gwen . . . oh Gwen,*" it seemed to say.

Gwen immediately sat straight up. "Noelle," she whispered, "do you hear that?"

Noelle sniffed and rubbed her nose, looking at Gwen quizzically. She shook her head.

"I heard something . . . " Gwen rubbed the tears from her eyes and strained her ears, desperately listening.

As the girls grew quiet, they realized they could faintly hear the sound of another woman crying.

"*Where are you, Gwen?*" the voice quietly moaned. Gwen suddenly gasped and clasped her hands over her heart.

"Mom!" she exclaimed. "Mom!" She looked at Noelle, utterly confused. "Noelle, that's my mom's voice! I am sure it is!"

Noelle looked closely at Gwen, feeling just as confused. They were definitely alone in the room. Suddenly, her eyes lit up and she grabbed at the golden shell still hanging from her neck. "Gwen, the shell!" She held it up and Gwen peered closely at it.

"*Oh my sweet Gwen, where have you gone?*" her mother's voice wept from inside the shell.

"Gwen, did you leave the oracle's enchanted shell behind?" Noelle asked. Gwen nodded, her eyes wide and her heart pounding at the sound of her mother crying. "Then the enchantment still works! Your mother must have found it!"

Gwen gasped and clutched the shell that Noelle held out, holding it close to her mouth. "Mom?" she called into it. "Mom? Can you hear me?"

She heard an audible gasp come from inside the small, delicate shell. "*Gwen? Is that you?*"

"Mom! It's me! Oh Mom, I'm here!" Gwen cried, her hands shaking and her mind racing. "Mom! Look for the golden shell on my window!"

"*Gwen?*" Her mother's voice was suddenly much louder, though still somewhat muffled.

"Mom, it's me! You can really hear me?" Gwen cried into the shell.

"*I can hear you, Gwen. But . . . but I don't understand,*" her mother stammered. "*Oh Gwen, I have been looking everywhere for you. I have been so scared.*"

Gwen felt waves of sadness crashing inside of her. The sound of her mother's voice made her heart swell with so much love and longing that she thought it would burst. "Mom, I miss you so much. I didn't mean to leave you like I did. But, I just had to leave. I don't know how to explain it . . . " She paused and looked at Noelle.

"*Where are you? Are you safe? How can I hear you?*" Her mother's panicked voice came through the shell.

Gwen shook her head. "Mom, I can hardly explain where I am, and no, I am not safe, but I had to do the right thing, just like you and Dad always taught me to do. She needed my help, Mom. I had to try to help . . . " Gwen's voice trailed off into a helpless whisper.

"*Who needed your help? What do you mean, Gwen?*"

Gwen kept one hand on the shell, and with the other took Noelle's hand and squeezed it. "Her name is Noelle, Mom, and she came to me for help."

The mermaids heard Grace catch her breath from within the shell. "*What . . . what did you just say?*" she whispered, her disbelief clear despite the ocean between them.

"I said her name is Noelle. She found me, Mom, and called to me from within that shell. That's how we're talking now," Gwen tried to explain.

"*You're with . . . Noelle?*" Grace whispered again.

"Yes, Mom. She's here. She's . . . well, it's very hard to explain. But she's wonderful, and I trust her, Mom. And I'm trying to help her," Gwen said, not at all sure how to describe her situation to her mother. She looked desperately at Noelle.

Noelle tilted her head toward the shell cradled in Gwen's hands. "Hello," she said softly.

"*I . . . I . . . Noelle?*" Grace stammered.

"Yes, my name is Noelle. And I am with Gwen," Noelle whispered into the shell.

The mermaids were only answered by the sound of Grace sobbing.

"Mom? Mom, are you alright? What's wrong?" Gwen cried.

"*I don't know what is happening. I can't lose another daughter. I can't go through this again. And I never . . . I never thought I would hear that name again,*" Grace sobbed.

Gwen sat up straight, her back pressed against the cold dresser. Another shiver ran down her spine. What was her mother talking about? "Another daughter? Mom, what do you mean?" Gwen looked at Noelle, who seemed just as confused as her.

"Gwen, you were so little, you don't remember. And I never could find a way to tell you," Grace's heartbroken voice sobbed through the shell. *"You had a sister, a baby sister."*

Gwen and Noelle both gasped. "What?" Gwen cried, her mind spinning.

"She was so beautiful, Gwen. She had the same blond hair and blue eyes that you have, and she was the sweetest baby. We loved her just as we love you. And . . . " Grace's voice broke for a moment.

At the same time, the mermaids felt a push on the door behind the dresser. "In here, my lady!" a serpent voice hissed. "I found them, my lady!"

Icy dread filled Gwen's heart, but she was less concerned about the serpents than she was about her mother's voice, being carried to her from the dry world far above the underwater room in which she was trapped.

"And what, Mom?" she whispered into the shell.

" . . . and her name was Noelle," Grace said, her voice shaking with tears and emotion.

Gwen and Noelle both froze, looking into each other's blue eyes. They felt another push on the door as the snakes tried to break into the room.

As if in a dream, Gwen whispered, "I had a sister named Noelle . . . "

"She was stolen from us in the nighttime when she was just a baby, Gwen. Gone without a trace. We spent years searching for her, and never found her."

"And that's why we moved to the sea. You said you felt drawn to the sea . . . " Gwen breathed, still looking into Noelle's wide, confused eyes.

"Yes, though I can't explain it. I never stopped looking for Noelle, my Noelle, but I knew I had to bring you and your brother to the sea," Grace said quietly.

"Could it be?" Gwen whispered. She squinted through the hazy water at Noelle, searching for the truth in her curly blond hair and her blue eyes. "Did I find you?"

"I found *you!*" the cruel voice of Mauvais cried out from the other side of the door. A great shuddering crack shook the door and the dresser, the only barrier between the mermaids and the wicked sorceress.

"*What was that?*" Grace's panicked voice called from the shell.

Gwen and Noelle held hands and swam to the other side of the room, as far away as possible from the door. There was nowhere else for them to go. But even as the threat of Mauvais loomed on the other side of the wall, the girls were instead thinking about what Grace had just said.

"Mom . . . I think I found her. I found Noelle," Gwen cried into the shell.

"*You . . . you mean . . .*" Grace stammered.

Gwen shook her head, helplessly confused. Noelle was a mermaid. How could she possibly be her sister? The blond hair, the blue eyes, the way she immediately trusted and cared for her . . . was it enough? How could she know for sure?

Suddenly Gwen's eyes looked at Noelle's shoulder. The birthmark! "Mom!" she called into the shell. "Mom, did Noelle have any kind of marks on her? Birthmarks, I mean?"

The door pounded again, and the dresser moved slightly across the floor. Mauvais's icy laughter filtered through the cracks appearing in the door.

"*Yes,*" the girls heard Grace say. "*Yes, she had a birthmark on one shoulder. It almost looked like a little fish.*"

Just as the door crumbled and Mauvais pushed against the dresser, Gwen and Noelle felt the fear that had been overwhelming them turn into genuine joy. Gwen let out a happy laugh, pulled Noelle into a loving hug, and shouted, "Mom! I found her! It's really her!"

They heard the sounds of sobs and stammerings coming from inside the shell, but at that moment Mauvais shoved herself into the room.

The mermaids turned to face her. Mauvais was giant. Her gray face resembled a human face, but was twisted with cruelty and malice. She had flashing dark eyes, and two sharp, curved horns where her ears should have been. Her long, spidery arms clutched a black trident, and instead of a mermaid's tail, she had four bloated, slithering tentacles. She wore a long, blood-red robe, and a matching red crown sat upon her head, holding back her flowing black hair.

Mauvais glided into the room on her oozing tentacles and her lips twisted in a wicked smile. "There you are, you sneaky little mermaids," she hissed.

Noelle's terror was gone, and she thrust Gwen behind herself, putting her own body between Mauvais and the long-lost sister she had brought under the sea. She kept hold of Gwen's hand, and as Gwen squeezed it, courage flowed between the two mermaids, whose love for one another was now stronger than their fear of the wicked sorceress.

Mauvais let out an evil laugh that seemed to boil the water around her cruel lips. "So brave, little mermaid," she taunted. "But once you're gone, there will be nothing stopping me from finally controlling this city. And once I control this city, I will control all of the Monde Aquatique!" She raised her trident menacingly and laughed again.

Noelle bravely shook her head and looked straight into the sorceress's flashing eyes. "You can do whatever you like to me, Mauvais, but you will *not* lay a finger on my sister!"

At those words, a tremor shook Mauvais's grotesque body. "What . . . what did you say?" The hand holding the trident dropped, and Mauvais squinted at the small mermaid before her.

Noelle, seeing Mauvais hesitate, said in a louder voice, "You will not harm my sister, Gwen!" She squeezed Gwen's hand again, and cried into the shell, "Mother, it's really me. I promise I won't let anything happen to Gwen! We will come home to you!"

"Noooo!" Mauvais shrieked, doubling over in pain and stretching out a crooked finger at Noelle. "How could you have found out?"

"*My darling Noelle, it's you? It's truly you?*" Grace's voice rang out from the shell. "*Oh Noelle, I love you! Gwen, I love you! My daughters, my beautiful daughters!*"

As Grace's loving voice filled the room, Mauvais howled in agony, and the water around her began churning. As Gwen and Noelle clutched each other, the sorceress began rocking back and forth, a whirlpool frothing around her. The water spun faster and faster, and Mauvais let out a terrible scream. "No, I won't be cast out again! I won't be . . . " Then, the water itself seemed to swallow the sorceress, and with a loud bang the entire whirlpool vanished.

Noelle and Gwen blinked, then stared, frozen, at the space where Mauvais had stood a moment ago. She was gone.

9

To the City Square

GWEN BLINKED AGAIN AND shook her head. The water, which had a moment ago been murky and foul, was suddenly crystal clear. Gwen could see for the first time the beautiful patterns of seashells decorating the dresser that now sat in the place where mere seconds ago Mauvais had stood menacingly. There was no sign of the sorceress, and the girls saw tails of the sea serpents as they fled from the room. Gwen watched them leave, and with a sigh of relief breathed in the pleasant smell of clean, salty water.

She felt Noelle squeeze her hand. "Is . . . is she gone?" Noelle whispered.

Gwen rubbed her eyes and looked once more at the empty room around them. "Yes, Noelle. I don't understand it, but she's gone."

"Girls, are you okay? What's going on?" Grace called through the shell.

"Yes, Mom, we're okay!" Gwen said. "We're safe!" She let out a laugh and threw her arms around Noelle, hugging her tightly. "We're safe now, Mom!"

Noelle laughed too. "My sister! I can't believe I have a sister! And a mother! I have a family!"

"And a father and a brother named Teddy!" Gwen exclaimed. "Oh Noelle, we can all be together again!" The girls looked into each other's shining blue eyes and grinned.

"*Oh girls, my girls, can you come home to me?*" Grace called out, her voice thick with emotion.

"Yes, Mom. And we have so much to tell you!" Gwen cried into the shell. At that moment, the mermaids started to hear the passageways outside of the room filling up with the merfolk of Sous-Marin. Jubilant sounds of laughter and celebration reached their ears as the city came back to life, rejoicing at the victory over Mauvais and her sea serpents.

Noelle let out a ringing laugh and said into the shell, "Yes, Mother, we will tell you the whole story, but right now we must go see my city. Come to the shore this evening, and we will come find you!" Noelle blew a kiss to the shell, and added, "I love you, Mother."

They heard Grace crying as she said, "*I love you, Noelle. I love you so much. Thank God Gwen found you.*"

"We will be home soon, Mom! Wait for us at the shore!" Gwen called out. "I love you!" She kissed the shell, then let it fall back to its place around Noelle's neck. The mermaids rose from the floor of the room, hand in hand.

"Come on, let's go see if everything is okay!" Noelle said, and the girls swam around the dresser and out into the passageway.

Gwen couldn't help letting out a happy laugh as she surveyed the scene around her. The clear water seemed to sparkle with the beauty of the walls, which before had been muddled by the murky curse. Instead of a gloomy atmosphere hanging over the city, she could sense a feeling of joy in the water, as the sounds of celebration reached her ears. Two laughing mermaids swam toward them down the passageway, their long hair flowing behind them and their dazzling tails swishing merrily.

"Colette! Isabelle! Is everything okay now?" Noelle called out to them. The happy mermaids swam up to Noelle and embraced her.

"Noelle! You're here! Everything is wonderful!" Colette cried, clapping her hands with delight.

"Do you see the water?" Isabelle added. She closed her eyes and breathed deeply, savoring the salty smell of the clean ocean. She laughed and opened her eyes, grinning. "Everything is back to normal!"

"What about the sea serpents? Are they gone?" Gwen asked.

Colette and Isabelle nodded wildly. "Yes, yes, they're gone!" Colette said. "And everyone from the safe-chamber is heading to the city square to celebrate!" she added.

"What are we waiting for?" Noelle laughed. "Let's go!" She grabbed Gwen's hand again and the group of smiling mermaids swam back through the twisting hallways.

As they made their way to the city square, Gwen continued taking in the beauty of the city, made new in her eyes by the crystal-clear water. They joined other merfolk merrily cheering and laughing as they swam. Nobody yet seemed to have an explanation for the change, but Gwen and Noelle discovered from several mermen that as soon as the curse was lifted the sea serpents fled from the city and back into the open ocean. The girls did not share with anyone their experience with Mauvais; they didn't understand it themselves, and wanted the council to be the first to hear it.

After winding their way through the city, Gwen followed Noelle onto an enormous open platform that was already filled with merfolk. "This is the city square," Noelle said to Gwen.

Gwen looked around. The square was built into the side of the city, and the floor was constructed entirely of blue, turquoise, and white stones curling about in intricate designs. There were free-standing pillars of marble standing throughout the room, with lush, leafy moss and seaweeds growing around them. In the very center was a large, round platform that rose above the crowd, clearly a stage of some sort. It was an open-water room, with no ceiling, so that the sparkling ocean water and all kinds of fish surrounded it. Gwen found it to be a vibrant place, full of life and joy, especially as she saw hundreds of merfolk embracing one another and celebrating.

Noelle hugged dozens of mermaids, expressing her thankfulness that the city was safe. Gwen smiled as she saw a chubby arm waving frantically at them from across the room. It was Rosalee, still clasped firmly in her mother's arms. Gwen and Noelle waved back, and saw the mother bow her head in a gesture of deep gratitude. They returned the bow.

Suddenly, Noelle gasped and cried out, "Odette!" Gwen turned to look at the merchild Noelle swam to, who was leaning against a smiling Delphine. She was a beautiful girl, with shiny black hair emblazoned with gems and shells. She had lovely brown skin, chestnut eyes, and a bright orange tail. As Noelle embraced her, the girl broke into a gorgeous smile and her laughter rang out across the square. Gwen followed Noelle, smiling with relief that this merchild seemed to be perfectly well.

"Noelle! I've missed you so much!" Odette cried, squeezing Noelle in a tight hug while Delphine wiped tears from her eyes.

"Odette, I missed you too! And my heart broke when I heard you were sick," Noelle said, holding Odette out with her arms so she could look into her eyes. "But . . . you don't seem sick now!" She looked up questioningly at Delphine, who smiled and shrugged her shoulders.

Odette nodded. "It was the strangest thing, Noelle. I had been sick for weeks. I couldn't swim. I couldn't move. I couldn't hardly talk, there was so much pain." Noelle winced. "But then," Odette continued, "all of a sudden, the pain was gone! And the water was clear! I don't know how it happened!"

Noelle laughed and pulled the merchild into another hug. "Thank God! I am just so glad you're okay!"

Gwen smiled and wiped a happy tear from her eye. Even though she couldn't explain how it happened, her only wish since the moment she entered the ocean had been to help Noelle and her people to defeat the sorceress, and somehow that wish had come true. Gwen's heart swelled with love and gratitude as she watched her mermaid sister smiling and laughing. The danger was past, the fear was gone, and Noelle's city was once more a place of happiness and love.

As Noelle and Odette continued speaking to each other, Gwen suddenly noticed a general hush falling over the crowds of merfolk. She looked around, and noticed movement on the circular platform in the center of the room.

"Noelle!" Gwen called, tapping on her sister's shoulder. "Noelle, I think that's the council!"

Noelle and Odette both turned around and followed Gwen's pointing finger. The seven members of the council were swimming onto the platform, their flowing purple robes easily identifying them from the rest of the merfolk surrounding them.

"It *is* the council!" Noelle whispered excitedly. She smiled at Gwen and Odette. "Now we'll find out what happened and what's going on!"

As Noelle turned back toward the council, she suddenly gasped in disbelief. "It . . . it can't be!" she stammered as her eyes squinted at the center of the room. Auguste and Pierre, the two largest members of the council, were helping an eighth mermaid ascend the platform. She appeared to be ancient, with a withered black tail and straggly white hair. Her face was a maze of wrinkles, and her knobby fingers gripped tightly to the mermen helping her swim. But as she reached the top of the platform and turned to face the crowd, her flashing red eyes were full of power and life.

The entire room of merfolk fell silent and stared at this shocking mermaid. Gwen, without taking her eyes off of the mermaid's red eyes, quietly whispered to Noelle, "Who is that?"

"That," Noelle whispered back in a shaky voice, "is the oracle."

10

The History Reversed

GWEN CAUGHT HER BREATH. *The oracle,* she thought. *But what is she doing here?*

Beside her, Noelle was shaking her head slowly in confusion and amazement. The merfolk surrounding them all wore similar looks on their faces. It was clear the people of the city knew who this ancient mermaid was, but never in their wildest dreams imagined they would lay eyes on her.

As the oracle situated herself, leaning heavily on Pierre for support, Gwen watched as Auguste raised his arms for attention. "Good people of Sous-Marin," he called out in his deep booming voice, "today is a day which shall always be remembered in our great kingdom's history." At the sound of his voice, the crowd of merfolk came out of its trance, and many mermen and mermaids let out a cheer. "Today, for the first time in centuries, we found ourselves in terrible peril. For today, none other than the Sorceress Mauvais breached our wall and entered our city," Auguste continued.

Gwen heard gasps and cries ring out all around her. "Mauvais?" she heard dozens of merfolk whisper in astonishment.

"Yes," said Auguste, "Mauvais herself was behind it all. The cursed water, the sickness, and the attack today." Gwen continued to hear the sounds of bewilderment and disbelief around her as the merfolk of Sous-Marin learned of the danger they had truly been in. She reached out to Noelle and took her hand. Noelle squeezed it, as both mermaids shuddered at the memory of their encounter with the evil Mauvais.

"But she has been defeated, and with her defeat, her wicked army of sea serpents fled in fear. Her curse has been lifted, and once again the waters of the entire Monde Aquatique are beautiful and healthy," Auguste boomed, and the crowd again burst into cheers and applause.

"Now," Auguste continued once the noise settled down. "I am sure you all have many questions. And that is why, for the first time in our kingdom's history, the oracle has come." He turned to face the ancient mermaid, and the entire crowd of merfolk bowed respectfully to the oracle. Gwen also bowed her head, realizing how extraordinary it was for this venerable mermaid to be here among them.

A silence filled the room, as the merfolk of Sous-Marin waited with rapturous attention to find out what the oracle had to say. At last, the oracle spoke in a deep, raspy voice. The first words she said were, "Where is Noelle?"

Noelle gasped and shook in complete surprise. All of the mermen and mermaids around her turned to look at her, with stunned looks on their faces. The oracle's flashing red eyes were fixed on her, and she watched as one of the knobby fingers beckoned to her. Noelle gulped, and whispered to Gwen, "Come with me." Hand in hand, the two mermaids slowly swam to the platform, with the crowd parting in awe for them as they moved.

When they reached the platform, Constance, one of the council mermaids, reached down and helped the girls up until they were face to face with the oracle. Gwen couldn't help but stare in wonder as she beheld the ancient face. Centuries of life were etched into the deep folds of her wrinkles, and her white eyebrows arched in a knowing expression. Despite her obvious age, her red eyes were brilliantly bright, and Gwen felt as though the oracle could see into her very soul with one glance.

To the girls' utter astonishment, the oracle bowed her head to Noelle. Then, she reached out one of her knobby hands, took hold of Noelle's smooth hand, raised it to her feathery lips, and kissed it.

"This mermaid has saved us all," the oracle said to the crowd. Noelle's jaw dropped in shock.

"I . . . I . . . what?" Noelle stammered, looking into the oracle's eyes with bewilderment, while her ears were filled with the joyous noise of the crowd cheering again. Gwen, though also confused, grinned, and she was overcome with love for her mermaid sister.

Auguste again raised his hands for quiet, and the merfolk settled down to hear what the oracle had to say.

"For the time of your fathers, and grandfathers, and great-grandfathers, and great-great-grandfathers, and longer, Mauvais hid in the waters in the very darkest depths of the ocean," the oracle's raspy voice spoke. "Hid, yes, but never slept. Her pride, her anger, and her hatred stewed within her and made the waters around her boil. She longed for power, and sought desperately for a dark magic to seize control over the Monde Aquatique. The sea serpents were her eyes and ears as she remained in the dark, uttering her wicked incantations and building her evil power.

"But she failed time and time again to break the barrier of light and love that this kingdom had," the oracle continued. "For centuries, she remained in the depths, foiled and frustrated by her inability to exact the revenge she believed this kingdom deserved. But," the oracle paused, looking deeply into Noelle's eyes, "eleven years ago, Mauvais finally discovered the answer she had been looking for. She realized that her dark strength alone would never penetrate the light. She had to find a way to bring sadness, anguish, and fear into the Monde Aquatique itself. *That* would be the key to breaking the barrier. *That* would allow her to finally wield her dark magic against our kingdom.

"And so," the raspy voice went on, "she dwelt on sorrow, and suffering, and once she truly understood pain, she found her answer." The oracle's eyes moved to Gwen, who caught her breath in surprise. "Mauvais realized there is no greater joy or love than that of a mother holding her baby, the new life she bore and brought into the world. What then would be the greatest sorrow?" The oracle's red eyes moved back to Noelle. "A mother losing her child. There could be no greater suffering than that."

With those words, Gwen felt a sharp pain stab at her heart. The memory of her mother sobbing through the shell was fresh on her mind, and Gwen knew that the oracle spoke the truth. She glanced at Noelle, but Noelle's wide blue eyes were locked on the oracle's flashing red eyes. Gwen looked back at the oracle's wizened old face, and listened.

"Mauvais had discovered the key. Now she just needed to find the right spell. She knew she couldn't take a baby from under the sea. It would be too easy to remedy; too easy to find the child and give it back to its mother. It had to be a child who would never be found again, who could never know its mother. Then, the mother's sorrow would be eternal, and would feed Mauvais and fuel her dark power. She needed an earthen child."

At this, Noelle's eyes grew even wider. She gripped Gwen's hand and squeezed it hard. The oracle nodded wisely and said, "Yes, she had to find a baby, a beautiful baby who would be the very joy of her mother's life, and she had to take it. Using the very darkest of magics, she projected herself above the water and followed the scent of love to the home of a perfectly happy family: a mother with two beautiful daughters, one of them a newborn baby. And," she said gravely as she stared into Noelle's eyes, "she took it. She spirited the baby away without a trace, and with her enchantments she transformed it into a mermaid and brought it under the water.

"The sorrow of the baby's mother followed her under the water, just as Mauvais hoped," the oracle continued, as Gwen and Noelle looked at her with shock on their faces. "She wrapped the baby in a bed of seaweed and floated her into the Monde Aquatique, knowing that the good merfolk would take her in and give her a home. What the merfolk couldn't possibly know was that by bringing this baby into their kingdom, they also brought in the seeds of sorrow and despair: the sadness of a mother and daughter separated that would never go away. It would take time for the seeds to grow, but Mauvais could wait. It gave her time to mobilize her army of sea serpents."

As Noelle listened, her heart sank and her lips mouthed the word, *mother*. The thought of the anguish her mother must have felt when she went missing was unbearable.

The oracle saw the look on Noelle's face, but continued with her story. "And so, the enchantment was in place. But no spell is perfect. As with all enchantments, there was one way it could be broken: if the mother ever found her baby, her joy would break Mauvais's dark power. She tried to ensure this would never happen by casting another spell that no soul under the sea could tell this baby the truth of her origins nor of the spell itself."

Noelle gasped with sudden understanding. "The riddle! It's why you had to speak to me in the riddle!"

The oracle gave Noelle a kind smile. "Yes, Noelle. And when the dark power had grown enough, Mauvais was able to enact her plan. First, she cursed the waters, bringing sickness and sadness into our kingdom. When that happened, I sent your name in a dream to the council, so that they would send you to me. I could not tell you directly what to do—the spell prevented me from doing so—but I could give you clues and point you to your sister."

Gwen suddenly laughed, and she felt all of the council mermen and mermaids smiling with her. "Noelle, I understand! It all makes sense! *Earthen, ocean, the two shall be rejoined in familial harmony.* That's us, Noelle! Earthen: me and Mom! Ocean: you! Reunited as a happy family!"

Noelle squeezed Gwen's hand and smiled. "Yes, of course! And . . . the second part of the riddle. *Once bonded, the history reversed shall finally end the wicked curse.* So, we broke the curse . . . " Noelle paused and turned back to the oracle, confusion still in her eyes. "We broke the curse just by discovering the truth? That we were sisters?"

The oracle smiled, her red eyes flashing at the mermaids. "There is no 'just' about that. It was no small thing. You undid the terrible deed. You replaced sorrow with joy. You replaced hate with love. You . . . you must have reunited with your mother, somehow, though that is the missing piece of the puzzle." The oracle shook her head. "I don't know how your mother found out about you, Noelle, for I couldn't lead you to her. Only to Gwen."

Noelle smiled and held up the shell around her neck. "But you did, Oracle. You did lead us to our mother! At the very moment that Mauvais had us trapped, our mother spoke to us through your shell. We heard her voice, and she helped us to discover the truth. She cried with happiness when she realized Gwen found me."

"And," Gwen continued the story, "when Mauvais was swooping down on us, Noelle jumped between us. She said she wouldn't let Mauvais hurt her sister. And when Noelle said that, Mauvais cried out in pain and then was swallowed up by a whirlpool . . . or something." Gwen smiled sheepishly at the oracle, finding it hard to truly explain the bizarre way Mauvais had vanished in front of them.

The oracle simply beamed and nodded her head. "Yes, then the history was reversed. Your mother's joy, her love, her happiness, bonded you back together and broke Mauvais's spell. And your own selfless act of love, Noelle—that was more than Mauvais could take. You defeated her with love, which is infinitely more powerful than hate. Once faced with your love, Mauvais didn't stand a chance. She has once more been banished to her cave at the bottom of the sea."

Noelle jumped in surprise at the sudden sound of applause and cheering that erupted from the room. She turned around, having nearly forgotten that she was on an elevated platform in front of her entire city. She saw grateful tears in the eyes of the council, and the whole crowd of merfolk was clapping, hugging, and blowing kisses at the mermaid sisters. Gwen smiled and fought back her own tears. She threw an arm around Noelle, who hugged her back.

Auguste signaled to Constance, who brought forth two beautiful tiaras from underneath her purple robes. She swam to Gwen and Noelle, and held out the tiaras. Gwen gasped as she looked at them. They were dazzling, with delicate strands of gold interwoven with precious pearls and opals.

As Pierre took them and placed one on each sister, Auguste's booming voice called out, "Good merfolk of Sous-Marin, we honor these mermaids today. Their goodness, selflessness, and courage in the face of the greatest danger will be remembered for centuries. They are the two little mermaids who saved our great city!" He smiled at the mermaids as a deafening cheer again sounded from the crowd. Pierre turned the girls to face the crowd, and they smiled and waved to the merfolk.

Gwen felt a great swell of love and joy inside of her. She had her sister, the merfolk were safe, and she knew her mother would soon be reunited with her long-lost daughter. She smiled, but a final thought suddenly struck her. How could her mother be reunited with Noelle? Gwen could remove her ring and become a human again . . . but what about Noelle?

The merfolk continued to cheer and applaud, and Noelle blew a happy kiss and then turned to Gwen. She immediately saw the look on Gwen's face and cried out, "Gwen, what's wrong?"

Gwen looked away from her sister's beautiful blue eyes, and instead stared at Noelle's glittering tail. She turned back to the oracle. "The history reversed . . . but, Noelle is still a mermaid. How can I actually reunite her with our mother?" she asked sadly.

Noelle's face fell as she realized what Gwen was saying. Somehow, even when Mauvais was defeated, she had remained a mermaid.

The oracle, however, looked at the girls with a twinkle in her red eyes. "I have brought you one final gift, little mermaid." Her knobby hand balled into a fist, which she raised up to Noelle. When she opened her fingers, a small silver ring etched with seashells sat on her palm. The oracle smiled. "When you put on this ring, Noelle, you will be transformed back into your human form. As long as it encircles your finger, you can live freely above the water."

Gwen and Noelle both cheered and embraced one another. Laughing, they twirled several happy circles, their tails swishing and their hair swirling. The room was filled with joy, as the merfolk of Sous-Marin soaked up the loving sight of the two sisters.

The memory of the curse was fading, and everyone felt safe and secure. The love, light, and joy of the city was back.

Auguste smiled at the mermaids and said, "With that, my dear Noelle, you know that you will always have a home here in Sous-Marin. You will be remembered forever, you and your brave sister Gwen." He put a strong hand on Noelle's shoulder and added, "But now, little mermaid, you can go home."

Noelle let out a ringing laugh, a laugh that put joy in the hearts of all who heard it. "I can go home! I have a family!" she laughed. Then she turned back to the oracle. "Do I understand you, Oracle, that as long as I wear the ring, I will be a human?" The oracle, smiling, nodded. "Does that mean . . . if I take the ring off, I will be a mermaid again?" The oracle nodded again.

Noelle turned to Gwen. "And Gwen, as long as you have the ring, you too can become a mermaid again! Oracle, does Gwen get to keep her ring?" she asked. The oracle said nothing, but nodded once more with a smile on her lips.

Gwen laughed along with Noelle. "Then this doesn't have to be goodbye, Noelle!" she cried. "We can always come back!" The sisters hugged again, laughing with joy at the realization that they could live in both worlds.

The oracle clasped the mermaids' hands, gave Noelle the ring, and bid them farewell. She bowed her head, and allowed the council to lead her back down the platform and through the crowd. Noelle carefully added the ring to the chain around her neck. As the council left the platform, Noelle was swarmed by groups of merchildren, who were all crying and begging her not to leave.

Noelle laughed and said, "It's not for forever! I promise I'll be back! I could never forget about you!" She hugged Odette for an extra moment, and then pulled back. She cupped the merchild's cheek in her hand and said, "I promise, I will come back." Odette smiled into Noelle's eyes.

Gwen and Noelle slowly made their way through the city square, stopping for embraces, kisses, and goodbyes. Noelle felt the emotion of leaving the city she loved, but the pull of being reunited with her mother was too strong for her to feel sad. She loved her life as a mermaid, and she loved Sous-Marin, but she knew where she belonged: with her family.

At last, the mermaids made their way to the edge of the city. Noelle turned around one final time and looked back at the underwater world.

"Are you ready?" Gwen asked, pausing with her sister.

Noelle's eyes scanned the beautiful city. She blew it a kiss, and then turned to face the ocean. She grabbed Gwen's hand and said, "Yes, Gwen. I'm ready. Let's go to Mom." The sisters smiled at each other, and swam out into the beautiful water, heading to the shore where their mother was waiting for them.

THE END